ALONE

ALONE

THE GIRL IN THE BOX, BOOK 1

Robert J. Crane

ALONE
THE GIRL IN THE BOX, BOOK 1

Robert J. Crane
Copyright © 2012
All Rights Reserved.

Acknowledgements

I've heard it said that writing is hard. I disagree; writing novels is easy thanks to the people I have to help me.

Once more, my greatest thanks to my editorial team:

First of all Heather Rodefer, a real trooper, who pores over each page with ruthless precision, purple pen in hand. Her tireless efforts, real-time feedback, and fearlessness in telling me when something is simply not working help keep my work from becoming self-indulgent codswallop.

Second, I must thank Debra Wesley, who in addition to being the speediest to deliver her feedback, is also a constant source of wry humor, insight into the larger world of fantasy and sci-fi, and affirmation for whatever project I've just completed.

Third, Shannon Garza read through this particular volume multiple times, trying to figure out what grammatical sin I had committed that caused her Texan sense (it's like spider-sense, but for Texans) to tingle with displeasure. She ended up figuring out by pure instinct something that I thought I had fixed. Kudos to her for helping me smoothe out that particular problem and also for finding the cover art after a long search on shutterstock.com.

I shudder to think what any of these books would look like without the countless hours these three put in helping me fix the errors of perspective and thought, grammar and syntax. Keeping a story straight in my head is a lot of work and it'd be impossible if not for outside help like theirs.

Thanks again to Kari Layman for the affirming conversations that led me to go out on a limb and write this book. If she'd said it didn't sound that interesting, I probably would have worked on something else and Sienna Nealon might never have left her house.

Thanks also to Calvin Sams, who read through and gave some very helpful notes.

A special shout-out and thanks to Nicholas J. Ambrose, author extraordinaire. You can find a sample of his new novel, Samantha's Promise, in the back of this work – and I recommend reading it, then buying the book.

The cover of this book is a (slightly cropped) photo by Anna Omelchenko, who I believe is in Lebanon.

To the fans, the people who have been buying and reading my work and sharing your feedback, a hearty, hearty thank you. The best letters always seem to come on the days when I need them most.

And finally, thanks to my family – wife, kids and parents – for doing all that you do so that I can do what I do.

One

When I woke up, there were two men in my house. As alarming as that would be for most girls, for me it's doubly so; no one but Mom and I are allowed in our house. No one. That's rule number one.

I sensed them creeping around in the living room as my body shot to instant wakefulness. It probably sounds weird, but I could hear them breathing and an unfamiliar scent filled the air, something brisk and fresh, that brought with it a chill that crept into my room. They did not speak.

I rolled off my bed, making much less noise than either of them. I crouched and crept to the doorway of my room, which was open. It was dark; dark enough for me to tell they were having trouble seeing because one of them brushed the coffee table, causing a glass to clatter. A muffled curse made its way to my ears as I huddled against the wall and slid to my feet. We had an alarm, but based on the fact that a deafening klaxon wasn't blaring, I could only assume they must have somehow circumvented it.

I didn't know what they were looking for, but I'm a seventeen-year-old girl (eighteen in a month, and I guess I'd say woman, but I don't feel like one – is that weird?) and there were two strange men in my home, so I guessed their motives were not pure.

How did they get in? The front door is always locked – see rule number one. I peeked around the doorframe and saw them. The one that hit the coffee table looked to be in his forties, had a few extra pounds, and I could tell, even in the dark, that he had less hair than he wished he did.

The other one was younger, I guessed late twenties, and his back was turned to me. They were both wearing suits with dark jackets, and the older guy had shoes that squeaked. Most people wouldn't notice, but right then I was hyperaware. He put a foot down on the linoleum in the kitchen and when he went to take another step there was a subtle sound, the squeal of rubber soles that caused those little hairs on my arm to stand up.

I weigh a hundred and thirty-seven pounds and stand five foot four. The old one was over six feet, the younger a little taller than me. The young one held his hands in front of him, probably because his eyes still hadn't adjusted.

What do you do in a situation like this? I couldn't run; I'm not allowed to leave the house. That's rule number two, courtesy of Mom. So when she's at work, I'm at home. When she gets home from work, I'm at home.

I don't leave the house, ever.

The two of them edged their way around. The old fat one stepped on a soda can and swore again. I was suddenly thankful for my pitiful housekeeping efforts of late. I saw the younger one heading toward me, and wondered what to do. Can't leave. I reached to my right and felt the press of an eskrima stick in my hand, leaning against the old record player. I picked it up and transferred it to my left hand while my right went back to searching for its companion.

Eskrima sticks are batons, each about two feet in length. I could fight with one alone, if I had to, but I'm better with two. Mom started teaching me martial arts when I was six. I'm only allowed to watch an hour of TV a day, and that's if I do all my chores, all my studies, and I've behaved myself. The eskrima sticks are part of my studies. Two hours of martial arts every single day, no exceptions.

The young guy peered through the door and didn't see me. I was huddled against the wall, motionless, crouching at waist level for him. He swiveled when I moved but before he got a chance to react, I brought the eskrima stick up into his groin. I didn't know him or what he was here for, so I didn't swing with full force, but it still ruined his day. Just like Mom taught me.

He let out a scream and I rose, driving the point of my shoulder into his solar plexus – that's the place in your stomach where if you get hit, you'd say you got the wind knocked out of you. Wheezing and gasping, it sounded like he was going to get sick on me. Mom says that happens sometimes, so I moved out of the way as he fell to his knees. An eskrima stick to the back of the head put his lights out. As he fell, I caught a faint whiff of a pleasant scent – sweet yet pungent, cologne of some sort I guessed. It was unlike anything I'd ever smelled before. I liked it.

A stream of curses reached my ears from Oldie in the living room, and I saw his hand come through the door, so I reached out and made a connection with his wrist – with one of the sticks, of course. Just a tap. He yanked it back with a grunt of pain. I flung myself through the door, leading with a front kick that he blocked with the same hand I had just whacked, and he grunted again before trying to counter with a punch.

He was pretty far away, so I let him follow through. I didn't think he could see me, and he was as slow as a glacier compared to Mom. She practiced with me every day, and still beat the hell out of me during practice. You'd think after training with the woman for twelve years I'd have figured out how to beat her, but no...

Oldie took another swing and I sidestepped, my feet carrying me into the kitchen. I brought the eskrima stick overhand and cracked him on the head as I let out a little giggle. I couldn't help it, really. Day after day it was study, study, study, practice, practice, maybe watch a little TV, wonder why I'm not as good at fighting as Mom, and then one day you wake up and there are two men in the house. And I'm beating them both senseless without giving it my full effort.

What does it say about me that I haven't seen a living human being other than Mom in twelve years and my first instinct is to knock them unconscious?

I'd worry more about it, but Mom's been gone for over a week – coincidence that these guys show up now? Mom comes home every day after work. Set your watch by her: with only an occasional exception, she was home at 5:34.

But I haven't seen her in a week. I thought about leaving, but what if it's a test? There was an alarm, after all; she could have been monitoring, and then I'd fail the test – and that would be bad. We'll define "bad" later.

After I giggled, Oldie whirled away from me. I pursued, and to the old guy's credit, he dodged pretty well. Of course, I was holding back. Not sure why. Mom would have been pissed that I wasn't attacking full out. I landed another eskrima on his chin and he staggered back and caught hold of the curtain in the dinette, yanking them off the wall anchors as he fell.

And thus violated rule number three: don't open the curtains or look out the windows. Most of them in the front of the house have heavy dressers and furniture blocking them, and all of them have bars on the exterior. The ones in the rear open to a backyard that has a fence eight feet tall all the way around and lots of old trees that pretty much blot out any view of the sun.

Don't think I'm a perfect goody-goody – I've snuck a look out back lots of times. My conclusion – it's a big, bright world out there. Really damned bright, in fact. Blinding.

I would have kept after him, but when the curtains fell the daylight streamed in and I couldn't see anything for a few seconds. When my eyes recovered I found the old guy throwing the curtains off himself and he came up with a gun in his hand. I guess I shouldn't have taken it easy on him.

The first shot would have gotten me in the face if I hadn't

already been moving. I dodged behind the couch as the shot rang out. Then another and another. They were loud but not deafening. The microwave in the kitchen took the first two; the next three hit the sofa and I heard the muffled impacts as stuffing flew through the air. I was crawling my ass off, heading for the door. I dodged under the coffee table, the one Oldie had hit on his way in, rolled onto my back and put my feet and hands on the underside of the glass.

I saw him emerge from behind the sofa and knew my time was limited. His gun was pointed at me, so I flung the table at him with my hands and feet. Kinda ugly, but it knocked him off balance as the glass shattered in his face and I heard the gun skitter from his hand back toward the dinette.

I didn't take any chances; I was on my feet in a second and sprinting toward the front door. He got the gun back as I was making my escape and I heard three more shots impact behind me as I slammed the door to the porch. I reached down and hit the outside lock – I know it sounds weird, but I locked them in my own house. Locked them in, and me out.

For those of you keeping score:

Rule # 1 – Mom and I are the only ones allowed in our house.

Rule # 2 – I am never to leave the house.

Rule # 3 – Never open the curtains or look outside.

Sorry, Mom, I thought. *We're just breaking your rules all to hell today*. I heard the gunfire again and I ran, dodging out the front door of the porch. I'd seen this space a thousand times as Mom was leaving, but never what lay beyond it. My hand flew to the knob that opened the door that led to the outside world.

If it had been up to me, I might have wanted to reflect on what a momentous day this was, going outside for the first time in twelve years; on violating so many rules, the first three big ones, all in a five-minute period. As it was, the sound of gunshots chased me into the light of day.

The cold hit me as I ran out, breath frosting as it hit the air. Fortunately, I'm always fully dressed – down to having on gloves all the time. That's rule four – always fully dressed, always long sleeves and pants, and always have your gloves on. I've asked why and Mom has declined to explain, answering with a simple, terse, "Because I said so."

I guess it was in case I ever had to run.

My eyes scanned the landscape of the suburban street in front of me. Even though the sky was covered in clouds, it was bright. The smell of the air crept up my nose along with the cold, and it felt like the inside of my nostrils froze. It was beyond crisp, and it almost hurt when I inhaled it. The frigidness bit at me even through my turtleneck sweater, and I found myself wishing for a coat. The wind blew down the road in front of me – rows of ordinary houses, idyllic and snow covered, trees in the front yards, draped in a blanket of winter white.

I slipped on the front walk and felt my heart kick me in the chest in a sensation of gut-punching fear. My hand caught me and I bounced back to my feet. *So that's ice?* I thought. Until now I had only seen it on TV and in the freezer. There was a black sedan in the driveway that looked like something I'd seen on a Buick commercial.

My hand brushed against it as I ran down the driveway and stopped at the end. I heard the sound of more gunshots and ducked behind the car. Clinking noises came from behind me as the shots bounced off their vehicle. Now what?

As if to answer my question a red SUV skidded to a stop in front of me. A small line of muddy snow splattered past me as the passenger door opened. Inside was a guy. Dark brown hair hung around his shoulders and his skin was tanned; I was not too flustered or in too much of a hurry to realize that he was not bad looking. His eyes broke the distance between us as he stared me down. His black coat ruffled from the open door and I heard his voice, raised to a pitch, and he spoke – something that should have sounded like a command, but was so gentle it came off as an invitation.

"Get in."

Two

I looked back and saw Oldie coming around the edge of the car. He had the gun up and pointed, and was almost to me. My only thought was – *Damn, he's slow*. I blasted him with a roundhouse kick, minding my footing, and made solid contact, kicking his arm aside. I stepped in and delivered an elbow to his midsection, bringing my hand around with a perfect twist to pull the gun from his grasp. With a last effort I brought my knee up to his gut and then dropped him with an elbow to the back of the head.

He landed on all fours and grabbed at my foot, so I whipped him in the top of the head with his own gun, sending him facedown into the slush on the driveway. I turned back to the handsome man in the SUV and pointed the gun at him.

"Still want me to get in? Now it's on my terms."

His hands rose in surrender and a slight smile twisted the corner of his mouth. "Yes."

I got in and shut the door. "Where to?" I kept the gun pointed at him.

Brown eyes stared back at me, the color of the dark cherrywood our kitchen table was made of. "Where would you like to go?"

"Away."

His lips turned into a full-blown smile. He stomped on the pedal and we started moving. I'd seen a car move on TV, but it was nothing like the real thing. I felt the acceleration push me back into the comfortable seat. The whole car smelled good, with an aroma I couldn't define but that reminded me very vaguely of the times Mother would bring home flowers on special occasions.

My eyes stayed on him, even as we turned a corner. I darted a look out the window and then back to him. He kept that same faint smile but he watched the road. Houses passed us on either side in a blur of colors overwhelmed by the white of the snow. We shot through an intersection and the traffic light made me stare. I turned back to him. "What's your name?"

He looked over at me for a flicker before turning back to the road. "Reed."

I nodded. It was a nice name. I was suddenly conscious of the fact that Mom must surely have had a rule against talking to strangers, but we never discussed what to do if you're driven out of the house by men with guns. My hand ached where I had landed on it after my slip. "I'm…Sienna."

"Nice to meet you, Sienna." He moved one of his hands off the wheel and proffered it to me.

I shook it. "Thank you." It was the first time I had been out of my house since I was five years old. I hadn't talked to another human being besides Mom for that long. I wondered if this was how people talked? Had conversations?

"Where should we go?" His hands gripped the steering wheel tight, and I could see the knuckles of his darker skin turn white from the pressure.

My head was still spinning from all that had happened in the last ten minutes, but I had an idea. "Somewhere public. With lots of people. A grocery store."

"Fair enough."

We rode in silence. I studied him, looking at the lines of his face. He couldn't have been much older than me. Other than through TV, I hadn't seen another living soul in years except Mom. When your only human experience in life is through the TV, it warps your sense of reality. The people on TV are so flawless that you don't see the little blemishes on the skin; the little mole below his eye, the freckles that barely showed on his cheek.

We pulled into a parking lot and I marveled at the size of the sign out front. I stepped out of the car and the bite of the chill hit me. My black turtleneck didn't do much to protect me against the deep freeze that was the outdoors. I knew it had to be cold outside from the draft through the windows at home, but I didn't know it was this cold. My leather gloves felt like they weren't even there and the clouds covered the sky above, bathing the scene before me in a dull light.

The melted snow under my feet in the parking lot surprised me. Now that I wasn't having to run, I took my time, listening to the oozing, splashing sound it made as I brought my shoes down into it, then felt the cold of the icy slush go into my socks. I cringed. Not exactly how I pictured my first time out of the house: I assumed I would run barefoot through a meadow, with the sun shining bright above, the warmth on my skin, bright colored flowers and green fields around me. Silly, clichéd, I know. But that's what I wanted.

If I ever could have gotten out of the house.

We walked to the front doors and they parted for us. An involuntary grin split my face. Very cool.

Reed laughed. "Never seen an automatic door before?"

"Nope." I stared at them, almost afraid that if I took my eyes away they'd vanish and I'd be back in the house, alone and dreaming.

"Come on." His hand wrapped around my upper arm with a gentle pressure and I felt a slight tingle as he guided me inside – not pushy or demanding, but with…care. I could feel the warmth of his hand through my sweater and the weight of the gun in the front waistband of my jeans. The heated air of the store blew down on me as I walked through the entry, a pleasant feeling to counteract the chill.

We stopped inside and the smell of roasting chicken hit my

nose. My mouth started to water; Mom hadn't shopped for at least a week before she disappeared. Last night I picked at the remainder of what was in the fridge. It was a little desperate; I was over ramen noodles and ketchup.

A big counter of clear glass stretched across the wall of the store. I could see a huge selection of meats and cheeses waiting inside it. My eyes wandered to the big freezers with boxes and bags of food, and I felt like I was going to start drooling. There were booths arranged near the deli counter – like a restaurant right there in the store.

"You hungry?" Reed's eyes found mine and I nodded. "I'll buy you lunch."

I stopped him. "Why are you being so nice to me? It's not like you pick up strangers on the side of the road every day who have someone pointing a gun at them." I paused. "Or do you?"

He blinked. "It's not a usual thing. But you have to understand…there are a lot of people looking for you."

"For me?" A doubt caused me to shiver. I hadn't believed he was someone driving by my house at random, but having the gun made me feel like I was still in control when I went with him. Still, it worried me when he confirmed what I suspected.

"Yes, you." He looked to either side. "Let me get you something to eat. I doubt you have any money."

"I don't."

He bought one of the big chickens that came in a cardboard box. I ate without consideration for how it looked, and he watched.

"Who are you?" I asked him between bites.

"Reed."

"Smartass." I glared at him, but it lacked intensity. I had a hard time being mad at someone who was feeding me.

He shrugged. "It's true."

"Beyond that."

"Someone who's concerned about you." His face grew serious. "There are dangerous people after you, Sienna."

"How do you know?" I sighed. "Beyond the obvious fact that they shot at me."

He hesitated. "Those guys…the young one's name is Zack Davis; the older one is Kurt Hannegan." He must have seen me stiffen in surprise, because he leaned back from the table. "I wasn't sitting outside your house by coincidence."

I felt the flush of blood running to my cheeks. "Are you with them? Are you one of them?"

"No." He shook his head, hot with indignation. "I'm not. But there are worse things after you than those two."

"Who are they?" I asked. "Who are you?"

He placed his palms on the table. "That's not the question you should be asking."

"Oh?" My eyes narrowed. "What question should I be asking?"

"The question you should ask is 'What am I?'" His eyes darted left and right. "Do you think it's normal for a mother to lock her child in a house and not let her out for years? Even in your limited experience, that can't seem quite right—"

"Mom said it was for my own good—"

"I bet," he interrupted. His face barely concealed disdain. "Putting that aside, I know your mother disappeared—"

"How do you know that?" My fingernails dug into the soft wood surface of the table, leaving marks. "Do you know where she is?"

"No. But she goes missing and suddenly you have a host of people after you?" He wasn't smiling. "You realize that's not coincidence."

"I do. I'm not stupid."

"Didn't say you were. I—" He stopped midsentence and his eyes widened as he looked past me. I turned my head to follow his gaze as Oldie walked in through the sliding doors with a thin young guy at his side – the guy I had hit in the groin earlier. He was limping. And he was hot.

"How did they find me?" I turned to Reed, and he wore a stricken look.

"Some sort of tracking device, maybe," he murmured, sliding out of the booth. "Let's get out of here."

"Nuh uh. I want answers." My hand slid to my waistband. Mom had taught me the basics of how to use a gun, though I had never fired one. Tough to practice shooting live rounds in the house.

His eyes almost exploded out of his skull. "Are you crazy?" His voice was just above a whisper, but it was delivered with the force of a shout.

"I bet they know about my mom."

I started to advance on them, but he brushed against my arm. I looked to his eyes, and they were wide with fear – for me. "You don't know what they're willing to do." He tugged on my arm. "Please. Let's leave before they see you."

The gears were grinding in my head. I'd been left alone for a week, and these guys came for me, armed. Mom was missing and I didn't know where she was. Lots of questions. I looked back at him and a hint of pleading was obvious in his brown eyes. Seeing the world on TV was different than seeing it like this. And for some reason I couldn't define, I trusted him – a little. "All right. Let's go."

We watched as the young man (so tempted to call him Hottie) and Oldie split up, each headed in a different direction to search the store. We waited until Oldie had walked down an aisle and Hottie had his back turned before making our move. We walked out the entrance door and into the parking lot, and Reed's pace quickened. The snow sloshed beneath us and the cold bored into gaps in my clothing that I didn't know were there.

As we approached his car, I looked up. The sun was still hiding behind the clouds; I had yet to see it. I looked over my shoulder. The two stooges weren't following us. I turned to Reed to make a wisecrack and stopped, my mouth agape.

A monstrous hand with long, pointed fingernails was wrapped around Reed's throat. His olive skin was turning purple and there was no sound coming from his mouth, which was open. His eyes were locked on me and his hands were wrapped around an arm that looked bigger than my torso. My eyes followed the arm to a man, at least a foot taller than me, built thick and muscled like a pro bodybuilder.

His head was huge, hair tangled and matted, dark with streaks of gray running through and it almost covered his brow. Furrowed above his black eyes were two eyebrows that were shaped like knife blades. His sideburns rolled down into a scraggly and unkempt beard that ran around his mouth.

Oh God, his mouth.

Pointed teeth. I've never seen anything like them – and his lips upturned in a cruel smile, his tongue lashing back and forth, not quite concealed by his incisors.

"Hello, little doll," he growled in a voice barely audible above the wind as he crept toward me. "My name is Wolfe. I've come to collect you."

Three

I felt fear creep through me; the sudden sickness for home that told me that I wasn't sure I was ready to be out in the world. It only lasted a few seconds, and then I brought down my right hand in a hammerblow against the weakest part of Wolfe's wrist.

And it bounced off.

Wolfe didn't even grunt in acknowledgment of my attack. He reached for me with his other hand – and I have to give him credit: he was *fast*.

I was faster. I swept in below his arm and rammed my head into his solar plexus. Not my ideal choice, but I was a little off balance and I didn't want him to get ahold of my neck. I slammed my forehead into his stomach, straightening my spine. I'd broken boards like this training with Mother, and it's not without discomfort.

He didn't react. My head felt like I had hit a wall where it should have been soft tissue. I spun to slide under his arm to get behind him, but the pain from my failed headbutt slowed me. He grabbed me around my turtleneck and lifted me off my feet as if he were picking up a head of lettuce one-handed. I felt the blood pooling in my brain, fighting to get out through the veins he had squeezed shut.

"Hey!" A voice drew my attention and Wolfe's. I was still struggling, but two men in their twenties approached wearing heavy coats and jeans. "What are you doing?" Their faces were contorted with rage and the one that was speaking pointed at Wolfe. "You can't treat a girl that way! Drop her!"

Wolfe acted as though he did not hear them and the two of

them rushed at him. I saw it coming through the haze that was beginning to cloud my vision, even if they didn't. Wolfe flung Reed into the side of a car and he ricocheted off, coming to rest in a pile on the ground. I would have worried about him if I wasn't too busy trying to free myself to take a breath.

Wolfe turned his body so that his left hand, the one he wasn't choking me with, could deal with them. His backhand sent the first flying a good six feet in the air and he landed with a crack on the asphalt almost fifteen feet away. It was so loud when he landed that it even caught my attention, and by this point sparkles of light were filling my eyes.

The second guy couldn't stop fast enough. Wolfe's hand lanced out, wrapping around the man's throat, but I could tell his grip was less merciful because the guy's eyes were bugging out of his head and Wolfe's fingernails had dug into his skin. Blood dripped down Wolfe's fingers, mixing with the spots in my vision. I hammered the bigger man's hands and wrists, searching for leverage, but I couldn't reach anything of importance.

By then things were so hazy it felt like I wasn't even in my body anymore. My hands relaxed and I stared into Wolfe's eyes, which were giant pools of black; no white, no iris, just black. I watched his hand relax and the Good Samaritan who tried to come to my rescue fell limp from his grasp. Blood was pooling in the snow and the man's eyes were open and lifeless. *Maybe if he'd had a gun.* The thought drifted into my mind.

A little shock ran through my brain. I had a gun.

My hand sprang to my waistband. I pulled the gun and brought it up as Wolfe licked the man's blood from his fingers. His eyes ran back to me as I pulled the trigger.

The shot hit him in the eyebrow and his hands flew to his face, releasing me. A howl as loud as an explosion threatened to overcome the sound of the blood rushing back to my head. I landed and my legs buckled. I fell to all fours, gun still clenched in my hand. I pulled up and shot at him twice more, this time aiming at his legs. My brain was sluggish, but when I looked to confirm that I hit him, all I saw was a thin black cylinder a little less than an inch long sticking out of the surface of his pants.

A dart was sticking out of his leg. Not a bullet wound. Damnation.

I raised the gun to shoot him again but his paw of a hand slapped it away. It skidded across the parking lot and under a car.

"Little doll," he breathed in my ear. I lifted my head up to see those great black eyes staring at me, but they were different, unfocused. "That's not a fair toy for playtime. What have you done to Wolfe?"

I might have responded if I'd had my wits about me, but his chokehold had deprived me of both oxygen and blood to the brain, and I was so dizzy I felt I might vomit. And if I did, I was aiming for him. Asshole. I was sucking down air greedily, large breaths so cold they hurt my lungs. It didn't seem to be helping. The spots were still clouding my vision. His eyes still stared at me.

"Back away from her!" I heard a voice from behind, but I was too gone to turn my head. Everything was spinning.

"New playmates are not part of our game," Wolfe breathed in my ear as he staggered to his feet. At least, I think he did. I saw his boots running through the snow, away from me.

I felt my head tilt back and my hair landed in the slush on the ground. I stared up into two faces – the men from my house. Oldie's swollen nose overshadowed his other features. They were both talking, but I couldn't hear a word by then.

The spots in my vision clouded everything out, and the spinning in my head worsened until it felt like I fell down, through the snow and slush and mud, through the concrete and asphalt of the parking lot, down into the ground. My vision darkened and blotted out the sky and faces above me.

Four

I awoke in a small room surrounded by sleek metal walls that reminded me of a stainless steel refrigerator, save for one that was made of glass and mirrored. If I went by my TV experiences, it was a one-way, and someone was watching me from the other side. The walls were paneled into squared segments that were two feet by two feet each, allowing the door to be disguised so I couldn't see the way out.

I lay on a hospital-style bed in the middle of the room. I had a moment of panic until I realized that my hands and feet were unbound. I sat up and dangled my legs over the edge of the table, then blinked down at them. I wore the same shoes that I had on when I was attacked. My gloves, sweater and jeans all seemed undisturbed. My hand jumped to my throat, checking where Wolfe had grasped me. Bandages covered my neck.

I walked to the mirrored wall, staring at myself. My brown hair highlighted my pale face. My blue eyes turned greenish toward the iris and my skin showed nary a freckle. Strange what twelve years with no sunlight will do to you. My nose was not quite pointed, but long enough to make me self-conscious. I wasn't sure what to think of my height or weight – it's hard to compare yourself solely to people on TV.

My fingers found the ends of the bandages wrapped around my neck and I pulled on them, gently at first, and then harder as they began to unwind. They were wrapped three layers deep, with only spots of crimson showing on the first layer, then heavier as I peeled them back until the last layer of gauze was covered in dried blood. I looked to my neck in the mirror and smiled. The skin was flawless.

"Impressive, isn't it?" A voice from behind caused me to turn, bandages already forgotten and hands at my sides, clenched and ready to move into a defensive position. The speaker was a stately woman in her forties, with bright red hair that showed not a streak of gray, bound into a tight ponytail. She wore a black jacket and pants that gave her the look of a businesswoman – not quite severe, but hardly casual. Her arms were folded in front of her and she wore only the thinnest hint of a smile. "You're Sienna Nealon." It was not a question.

She took a step toward me and the door behind her closed with a soft click. "You've been out for about a day and the wounds around your throat are gone."

"I heal fast." My words came out more acidic than I had intended. "Where's Reed?"

"He beat a hasty retreat after my men scared off Wolfe." Her eyes showed the first trace of amusement. "You should get better friends."

I studied her as she slowly cut the distance between us. "Can't say I wouldn't have done the same if I'd been mobile at the time."

She bowed her head and the smile became more than a hint. "That would have been a mistake. Because there's no one that can help you as much as we can." Her eyes rose to meet mine.

I laughed. Loud. "I haven't even heard who YOU are and now you're talking about a WE."

Her smile didn't dim a bit. "My name is Ariadne Fraser. I'm Chief of Operations for the proverbial 'we' – which in this case is called the Directorate."

My right hand found its way back to my neck and kneaded the new skin against the leather of my glove. "And what exactly is the Directorate?"

"We identify and assist meta-humans like yourself."

I felt my head spin, and I doubted it had anything to do with my recent injury. "What's a meta-human?"

She blushed. "A meta-human is someone like you – who has powers beyond that of a normal human."

"I have no idea what you're talking about."

"Your strength is far above a normal human's, my men tell me." She pointed at my neck. "I saw your wounds when they brought you in. Gouges like that don't heal in a day, and they leave scars. I'm sure you have other abilities as well. If you'd allow us to do some testing, we could help you—"

"And if I don't want your help?" I set my jaw and could feel my teeth clench. I didn't know where I could go, other than home – and I'd have a hell of a time finding it.

It was as if she could sense the uncertainty beneath my facade. "And where would you go?"

"Home. Where I was before your men broke in and forced me to kick their asses. Did you know one of them shot at me?"

Her elegant face crumpled in a frown. "Which one?"

"I don't know names. The old one."

Her frown deepened. "Kurt Hannegan. It was only a tranquilizer pistol—"

"Yeah, I found that out after I took it away from him, cranked a few rounds into Wolfe and he didn't die."

She took another step forward, reaching the bed I had awakened on. "Kurt and Zack were ordered to bring you here. Although I would have preferred that it had gone more smoothly—"

"Smoothly? They shot up my house and drove me out into the world, where a huge mutant squeezed my neck until my head nearly popped off!"

She grimaced. "I realize that it was your first exposure to the outside world in several years, and I wish—"

"Yeah, well, if wishes were horses I wouldn't need a ride

home."

She straightened. "You can't possibly be thinking of going home now. Not with Wolfe hunting you."

I glared at her. "I was doing just fine until your keystone cops broke into my house. Hell, I was doing just fine after they drove me out – and how do I know that this Wolfe guy isn't one of yours?"

"He is not—" she emphasized every syllable, ire running over her words—"one of *ours*. He is a monster, a killer by any definition, the type of threat we guard against. You must have seen – he killed two strangers in the parking lot."

Self-consciously, my hand played across my neck. Those men had been trying to help me, and they didn't even know me. "I saw it."

"You think we were involved in that?"

"Lady – Ariadne – whatever your name is, I don't know you. All I know is that my mom has been missing for a week, that your guys shot up my house—"

"With tranquilizer darts."

"—and then I meet one guy who says he wants to help me and another that grabs me by the throat and throttles me. Then I get brought here. I don't know any of you, I don't trust any of you, and I really just want to know where my mom is." The smallest dab of real emotion escaped me in my last words.

"I can help you with that – with finding her."

I paused in my tirade. "Do you know where she is?"

Ariadne deflated. "No. But we can search, and we have more resources to help with that than you do by yourself."

I smirked. "I'm sure you'd do that out of the kindness of your hearts."

"We're here to help meta-humans like yourself." Her fingers met and interlaced.

"And what do you want from me in return?"

She hesitated. "Nothing difficult. We'd like to run some tests—"

"Cut me open and prod my innards?"

"Nothing like that. We don't know what kind of meta-human you are."

I rubbed my eyes in fatigue and disbelief. "You keep calling me a meta-human. What is that?"

She straightened, portraying a certain pretentiousness as she lectured to me, the ignorant teenager. "Meta is from the Greek, meaning—"

"Beyond human. Yes, I know that." Her face fell and I was suddenly glad of the endless hours of study Mother had forced on me just for a chance to needle this woman who I'd known for less than five minutes but who already grated on me. "You were saying 'meta-humans' as though there are a lot of us."

Ariadne took a few steps away from the table and faced the mirror. I could still see her expression, and she looked up, as if she were recalling something. "There are six billion people in the world. By our estimates, less than three thousand are meta-human." She turned to face me. "Meta-humans have powers, skills and abilities beyond those of normal humans. Superior strength, speed and dexterity are usually signs of meta-human abilities."

"Is that all? Faster, stronger, more nimble?"

She shook her head. "Those are standard. Every meta-human has other, more unique abilities that manifest around age eighteen and are often hereditary."

Something clicked for me. "My mom was meta-human?"

A flash of surprise entered Ariadne's face. "Yes, she was - or is, depending on what's happened to her – meta-human, but we have no idea what type."

"How do you know about my mom?" My fists were clenched. I kept my eyes focused on her, trying to detect any hint she was lying.

"Your mother is a legend in our field," Ariadne replied. "She worked with the Agency – a precursor to the Directorate. It was the U.S. government's first attempt to monitor and control meta-human activity. She was a field agent, one of the best. She racked up an impressive string of captures of hostile meta-humans." Her expression softened. "She saved a lot of lives – human and meta."

"But she left?"

"The Agency was destroyed by a group of meta-human terrorists. Apparently she escaped before that happened, though it was assumed she hadn't survived the attack."

Understanding dawned on me. "You think she was involved?"

"She was with the Agency for ten years and disappeared at the same time it was destroyed? She must have been pregnant with you at the time, based on your age. So she disappears off the grid for over eighteen years if she's innocent?" Ariadne shrugged. "Maybe she was and she took the opportunity presented by the attack to escape to protect you. It is a dangerous line of work, trying to keep meta-humans under control."

"So you're with the government?"

"The Agency was. That's why they were found and destroyed. The Directorate is…not so encumbered." She smiled.

"Shady. So you want to test me?" I asked with more than a hint of suspicion. "Why?"

"There are different types of meta-humans. Let me start with some history. You've heard myths of giants, fairy tales, things like that? Meta-humans have been around as long as humanity, and humans described their abilities in ways that spread to become legend. For example, Wolfe." She took a deep breath. "He used to walk on all fours – I guess it's his preferred manner of movement; he looks—"

"Like a dog – or a wolf," I interrupted.

"Right, except he's one of three brothers, and – going by the word of a meta-human that's been alive for several thousand years – the three used to be guards for a Greek meta-human so vicious that he was known as Death. The brothers were called a three-headed dog at some point..."

"Three-headed dog..." I blinked. "...Cerberus?"

She cringed. "Appalling, isn't it? That's what several thousand years of folklore will do to the accuracy of a story. But according to our files, which only go back a century or so, he's killed hundreds, so he seems like the sort of hellhound that would guard the escape from the underworld, I suppose."

"And I'm like him in some way?" I felt a pang of disgust as I visualized the teeth of Wolfe.

Her voice became soothing, almost reassuring. "Like I said, there are different types of meta-humans. Wolfe is a creature who has built up a horrible legend, and he's lived for thousands and thousands of years. His proclivities for murder and torture are the stuff of serial killer stories." Her cringe turned to disgust. "He's a very powerful meta, but his homicidal tendencies put him on the fringe. I doubt you're anything like him." She shuddered. "I don't think anyone is – except maybe his brothers."

I tried to imagine three of them. One was plenty.

"About the testing process," she said. Her eyes bored into mine and I could tell she was trying to be caring or warm. It wasn't working. "We just want to help you find out what you are. If we had ill intentions, you would have woken up strapped to the table and the testing would have already been done. We're not here to hurt you or force you to do something against your will. We're here to help."

I thought about what she said. When I was unconscious, they could have violated me any way they wanted. Point in their favor, but I wasn't going to trust them that easy. "Noted."

"I don't expect you to make an immediate decision." She turned and indicated the place in the wall where she had entered.

"Now that we've talked, you're free to explore our campus and give it some thought. I've had quarters prepared for you; you can stay with us if you'd like."

I stared her down. "And if I don't like?"

She shrugged again. "Then you can leave. But I'd ask you to give it a day of thought first. Meet some of our people – including the meta-humans – and see what they have to say. With your mother missing, I doubt there's anyone else that could help you make your way through what must be a strange transition. Or protect you from others who would wish you harm."

I stuck my chin out in defiance. "What about Reed?"

"I don't know who he is or what his agenda is." I couldn't tell if she was lying or not. Damn.

"And how did you find me?"

I caught the strain of hesitation in her face. "We'd heard Wolfe was in the Minneapolis area, tracking the daughter of Sierra – your mother – so I sent Zack and Kurt to follow him. He led us to your house."

"Then why didn't he come charging in before your boys did?" My arms folded in front of me.

"They...sidelined him," she replied. "Shot him with darts that knocked him out while they entered your house to roust you."

"I see." I pursed my lips. "I'll stay – for a day. To...make up my mind."

A wan smile cracked her lips. "All I ask is that you give us a chance – to win your trust."

I returned her smile as she left, but as I turned my back on the one-sided mirror I felt it fade from my lips as I pondered her story about how they found me. I played back in my mind the expression on her face, the tone of her words as she told it. I considered how her eyes moved, darting back and forth.

That time, I knew she was lying.

Five

The snow stretched across the horizon. The Directorate facility was isolated and surrounded by rolling fields bordered by forests. The woods had evergreen trees as well as the seasonal ones that had lost their leaves. The winter had left the grounds settled under a couple feet of snow.

I sat on a bench behind the dormitory building. The Directorate campus was huge, dozens of buildings strung together by a web of interconnected paths that had been plowed and salted. After being shown to my room, I explored the closet and grabbed the heavy coat and gloves they had left and headed outside. After all, I had not spent any time outdoors in several years, and I took this, my first opportunity, to really look at and feel the snow.

I smiled as the wind swept over me, stinging my cheeks and chilling my nose. I felt the cold creeping between my toes in the thin boots I wore. The air was fresh; fresher than anything I could recall ever smelling, with just a hint of smoke from somewhere in the distance. I couldn't hear anything but the blowing of the wind. It was enough to make me forget that I couldn't go home and that even if I did, Mom wasn't there.

A memory sparked to mind, of us downstairs. Our house was old, with a basement that had concrete block walls, and pipes hanging everywhere. Mom had turned the largest part of it into a workout room, with mats on the floor for practicing martial arts. She had weapons hanging on the wall, and every day we'd practice for a few hours. She was good; she taught me everything I know.

And now she's gone.

I heard the footfalls behind me and turned. It was Oldie, Kurt Hannegan and his younger partner, Hottie. Zack, I remembered Ariadne calling him. They were both wearing their dark suits with black ties and looking solemn. In the light I could see them a little better. Kurt's nose was swollen from where I had hit him. Looking at Zack reaffirmed my suspicion that he was not hard on the eyes, and had sandy blond hair and a tanned face.

I had already gotten a look at Kurt when he was coming at me in the house. Big around the midsection, the waistband of his pants sticking out to wrap around his outstretched belly, giving him the look of a penguin. His face bore the scars of a long-ago bout with acne, and the little hair that remained on top of his head was thin and combed over from the bushy brambles that wrapped the sides of his skull. If he could wear a fedora, his baldness might be passable.

They both lurked just out of arm's reach. Zack looked at me and smiled, far more warmly than I deserved since a day ago I had hit him in the groin so hard I was surprised he was still walking. I felt a little tingle and looked away, straight at Kurt. Oldie glared, giving me a wary look you might reserve for a criminal offender.

"Nice to see you boys are up and walking," I said with a sarcasm that I couldn't get rid of, no matter how hard I tried. All right, I'll admit it – I didn't try very hard. But at least in Zack's case, I felt bad about it.

Zack spoke first, looking back at Kurt, almost for reassurance. "Yeah, you pack a mean punch with that baton." His eyes were brown, but I saw some humor in them. The forgiving sort? I pegged him for a sucker. One day out in the big, bad world and I could already spot them.

"Yeah, she's a real champ in the dark with a baton," Kurt shot back. "Step into the ring and lace up a pair of boxing gloves and we'll see what kind of fighter she is."

I smiled at him, a kind of dazzling, annoying, faux smile that probably set off his bullshit detector. He wasn't a sucker. "It wouldn't matter if it were drunken boxing, muay thai, kickboxing or just straight up, 'Marquess of Queensbury rules', because I could flatten your fat ass with any of those styles." I turned my head away to hide my smile but listened for footsteps in case he took umbrage and tried to sucker punch me. Even if he did, I would have bet I could still beat his ass.

Kurt's snort of indignation was drowned out by a chuckle and low whistle from Zack. The big man recovered. "I don't beat up little girls."

"You certainly don't succeed at it, but you try – and when that doesn't work out, you shoot at them until they take your gun away." I turned back in time to watch his face contort at my goad. My faux smile had turned real, an impish grin rooted in my deep amusement at twisting his tail. His little piggy tail.

Zack laughed again, a wheezing cackle that made him stoop to slap a knee. Kurt's face was ashen. "They don't pay me enough to deal with your meta crap. They should have sent M-Squad after you; I'm not a retriever—"

I smiled at him. "You should add that to the list of things you're not – a retriever, thin, a good shot, attractive, young, virile—"

He turned and stormed off in a perfect impression of countless divas I'd seen on TV over the years. I saluted his back as he walked down the path. "Don't forget 'possessed of a sense of humor' or 'gracious loser'!" He threw up a finger behind him as he continued his walk. "Oh! And 'witty'! You're not witty!"

"Damn," Zack said in mild consternation as he watched Kurt walk away. "I'm gonna have to soothe his wounded pride later." He turned back to me. "You really do pack a mean punch. Sienna, right?"

My smile went from mean-spirited to as pleasant as I could muster and I wasn't quite sure why. I guess there was no point in being wicked to everyone, especially not when Zack was trying to be nice. Besides, I'd already proven I could drop him to the ground if need be. "That's right. Sienna Nealon. You're Zack...?"

"Davis." He smiled. "You taken a tour of the grounds yet?"

I shook my head. "Saw the dormitory and the big building over there—" I waved in the direction that Kurt was heading— "that I woke up in."

"Yeah, that's our headquarters. But there's other stuff, too, like a gym, a garage and a firing range."

"A gym?" I cocked an eyebrow at that. The desire to work out was stronger than I would have guessed. I'd gone the week since Mom left without following the routine.

He shook his head, eyes wide. "I guess I shouldn't be amazed, but I kind of am. We brought you in less than twenty-four hours ago and I had to hold a jacket around your neck to keep you from bleeding to death. And now you're fine and looking for a place to work out." He pointed down a path and started walking. I fell into step beside him.

"You're not meta-human?"

He shook his head. "Just a normal guy. I work with them a lot, like M-Squad – they're all metas, and normally they'd be the ones that would have come to get you, not Kurt and me, but they're down in South America doing...something."

"Ooh, ominous."

He laughed. "Not supposed to be. They're probably bringing in another meta, but I'm not exactly in the loop, so I don't know for sure. That's what they do though; bring in new metas that we identify, or bring down ones that are causing trouble."

I eyed him. "And what I did yesterday, would that fit your definition of 'causing trouble?'"

He laughed again. "Nah, I would've fought back too if strangers broke into my house. We were supposed to bring you in quiet, and you metas don't typically do anything quiet if it's against your will. Kurt told 'em that, but Old Man Winter said to tranq you and be done with it."

I stopped walking. "Old Man Winter?"

He stopped and his tanned face adopted a pinched "I-shouldn't-have-said-that" look. "Ahh, I mean…damn. The boss."

"I thought Ariadne was the boss?"

He shook his head. "Ariadne's in charge, mostly, but she's not the big cheese. Old Man Winter…we call him that because…you know, some people say 'The Old Man' and he's kinda up there in the years, but he's…I dunno, cold. Like he never shows emotion. Never smiles, never gets angry."

"So you call him Old Man Winter. He got a name?"

"Erich Winter."

I laughed. "That explains it."

"Yeah. He's a good boss, just…"

"Cold."

"Right."

"So how long have you been with the Directorate?" I cast a sidelong glance at him as we walked. Ahead of us loomed a building that matched every other in the complex. Gray concrete walls, squat and blocky with a section that extended well above the rest of the building. Glass doors marked the entryway, but like all the others I had seen, it was unlabeled.

"Couple years. They got me coming out of the U of M."

"University of Minnesota?"

"Yeah. You gotta be close to college age. Were you thinking about going?"

I laughed. "You know my background, right?" He nodded. "Mom wasn't big on the idea of me leaving the house. Ever. Said it was dangerous."

His face turned serious. "She was right, you know. She kept you quiet all these years; now it's a rush to get ahold of you. Wolfe and whoever he works for – they're rounding up every meta they can lay hands on – and if Sierra Nealon's daughter is in play, it was going to be a mad dash to get to you first."

"What about the guy who saved me from you?" I looked at him as I asked the question, trying to see if he was as bad a liar as Ariadne. "His name was Reed. Do you know him?"

He shook his head with perfect sincerity. "I hadn't seen him before, but this isn't just a two-sided game. There's a lot of factions out there trying to get metas on their side."

"How did you know where to find me?" I eyed him and gave him a little smile. *So this is what it's like to play a man. Kinda easy.*

"I just go where I'm told." His smile was knowing. *Damn. Maybe it's not so easy.* "So, are you going to let Ariadne run her tests?" His voice quavered a little bit and I knew that it wasn't him asking this question.

I sighed, mostly for effect. Maybe it was because I'd never had the company of a man anytime in memory, but I was enjoying myself so much I almost forgot that I didn't have any friends, just a suspicious number of desirous and questionable "allies." "Maybe," I replied. "I'm still thinking about it."

"Tough choice, I guess." He sounded sincere. Maybe he was. "Your whole world gets turned upside down and you're left without anyone to rely on. Gotta figure out who's telling the truth."

I flashed him a tight smile, and I felt my heart beat faster than it should have after such a short walk. "Or figure out if nobody's telling the truth. You all have fantastic stories of meta-humans with amazing abilities, but so far the closest thing I've seen to the truth of that is a grubby mountain of a man that looks like he could have stumbled out of a pack of wolves."

Zack grinned. "It does sound kind of crazy."

"You're all saying that there are people with superpowers, and that I have one but no one can tell me what it is unless you 'test me.'" I rolled my eyes. "Forgive me for not jumping to sign up for that medical experiment."

His smile faded. "But...you realize how strong you are compared to a normal human, right?" He stopped as we neared the entrance to the gymnasium. "You realize how much more powerful you are?"

I started to suppress my instinctive reply but I was a half second too slow. "I don't know what to think. I don't know where to go. And I have no idea who to trust." *And I don't have idea why I told him that.*

He kept his distance and his hands slid into his pockets. I almost felt like he was doing it to avoid patting me on the shoulder or something. He took a step back to the concrete bench sitting in the shadow of the entry and did a double take as he looked down at it. "I can't help you fix all those problems. But maybe I can give you one answer." He pointed to the bench. "See this?"

"I may be meta-human, but I'm not blind."

His face twisted with a touch of condescension. "Nobody but Ariadne and Old Man Winter call them meta-humans. M-Squad just says 'metas' and it's kinda stuck for everybody." He leaned down and tried to push the bench. "It's a few hundred pounds, easy." His eyes glimmered with mischief. "Why don't you try lifting it?"

My stomach made a noise and I hoped only I could hear it. I walked over to him and studied the bench. It was concrete, with a nice pattern around the legs to give it some aesthetics. And Zack was right: it looked like it weighed quite a bit.

I reached down and grabbed hold by the edges. I cringed and counted down from three in my head and lifted with everything I had.

It flew off the ground and swung up, almost popping me in the mouth before I stopped it. I could feel the weight of it, but it wasn't that significant. I swung it around and hoisted it over my shoulder, holding it with one hand. "Wow."

"You never lifted anything like this before? Never tested your strength?" Zack kept his distance. I think he saw me lift it a little too aggressively and assumed (rightly) that I may be able to lift it, but I couldn't necessarily control it.

I shrugged, almost dropping the bench from my shoulder. I caught it and laughed. "What in our house would I have lifted?" I worked to keep a smile plastered on my face in spite of a sudden disquiet within as a memory of my hand pounding against metal, drawing blood, flashed through my mind.

"Odds are that your powers didn't manifest until recently anyway," he said with a shrug. "You might not have been able to do this a month ago. Metas I've talked to say it onsets over a few weeks or months...you just start getting faster, stronger, more agile than you used to be." My eyes glazed over for a moment as another memory floated to the top of mind. Zack looked at me with a quizzical expression. "What?"

I blinked. This one wasn't so bad. "A couple weeks ago, Mom and I were in the basement, sparring like usual. We trained martial arts a couple hours a day, and I've never been able to lay a hand on her. She's super fast, like a blur, and she always dodges. Always encouraging, you know – 'Keep it up, that's good, you came close there...'. But that time, a couple weeks ago, I thought she was a little slow and I dodged one of her kicks and tagged her in the ribs."

Zack nodded. "Ariadne and Old Man Winter said your mother was one of the most powerful metas in her generation. That's pretty good if you got a hand on her like that."

"Yeah..." I gazed off into the distance.

"What is it?" His brown eyes were rimmed with concern. Not an act, I think.

My eyes snapped back into focus and landed on him before I flicked my gaze away again. "Nothing...well...after I hit Mom, I was all flushed with victory. I took a step back; point scored, you know…formalities of sparring. I dropped my guard when I went back to my ready stance. She didn't even hesitate – she planted one on my jaw that knocked me off my feet and blurred my vision."

Zack physically recoiled and his eyes got wide. "That…that's horrible."

I felt the wind run through me and clamp down on my heart, pushing it into my throat. "No, it was good." I wiped any trace of emotion from my face. "She was trying to teach me not to ever let my guard down because it can cost you." The pain in my chest swelled as I pictured Mom's expression after she struck me down – fire blazing in her eyes; that look of spite and revenge all rolled into one as she looked down on me.

My mind raced, trying to think of something to ask Zack to change the subject. "You said my mom was one of the most powerful metas in her generation? So not all metas are the same, power-wise?"

"Yeah, there's a scale – some metas are stronger than others." He looked up at the bench still balanced on my shoulder. "That's why Ariadne wants to test you. Even without knowing what your other powers are, knowing your strength could give some insight into what kind of meta you are."

"Hm." I whipped the bench as if to smash it against the ground and noted the panicked look in Zack's eyes as he flinched and brought his hands in front of his face. I stopped it a few inches from the walk and gingerly placed it back where it had started and shot him a dazzling smile. "Fraidy cat."

He looked at me, eyes wide. "I couldn't tell you without testing, but seeing the way you handled that bench, I think you're right up there with your mom on the meta power scale."

I looked down. "I don't know about that. I fought back against Wolfe and he shook off my attacks and grabbed me like I was nothing."

"Yeah, but Wolfe is a freak of nature. Most metas don't live for thousands of years. He has."

"I don't doubt that, but he manhandled me. His strength was incredible; I couldn't fight back at all." I felt the bile rise in my mouth as I said that. Mom had always dominated me, but she'd never completely crushed me the way Wolfe had. It made me sick – and angry.

"He's THE top of the scale for power and he has millenia of experience fighting. He'd give M-Squad a run for their money, and they're all way up on the scale, and there's four of them." He shook his head. "I want you to promise me something."

I looked up at him and felt a tremble. "What?"

"You ever run across Wolfe again, do what the rest of us do – run like hell. He's a beast. And he will kill you."

Six

Zack showed me around the grounds and after we walked through more buildings and met more people than I could possibly remember, he took me to a four story brick building, a perfect square but with windows spaced every five feet on each floor. There were entrances at each corner. We walked into one of them to find the interior indicated it was a much older building than most of the others.

Yellowed corridors ran around the perimeter. They looked as though they might have been white when the building was built, but they had yellowed through time and use to the color of a boiled egg's yolk. The center of the structure looked to be one giant chamber and around the edge of the building a variety of labs were open to viewing by glass walls. "It's the science labs," Zack said.

"So this is where they cut me open?" I looked at him with a raised eyebrow.

"Not quite." A voice from behind made me turn. A small man with glasses and a white lab coat covering a shirt and tie came in behind us and stomped his feet. His hand came up to brush some snow off his shoulder and I saw no rings or jewelry on thin, delicate fingers that matched with his gaunt figure. He had zero hair on his head, not so much as an eyebrow, and wore the hipster-chic black rimmed glasses that seemed popular nowadays based on how many people wore them on TV. I think they look stupid, but in his case it might have been a clueless fashion decision.

"This is Dr. Ron Sessions," Zack said with an introductory

wave. "He's our chief science guru."

Dr. Sessions took a couple of strides toward me. "Is this Ms. Nealon?"

I looked from Zack to the doctor. "I'm Sienna, yeah."

His eyes lit up, and it was a calculating stare. "Ariadne sent me to look for you and here you are, in my humble halls."

"She wanted you to talk to me about the testing?"

He nodded a bit too eagerly. "Wanted me to explain the basics of it. It's a thorough process, so it could take a little while to go through and answer any questions you might have. Do you have some time now?"

I felt a gravitational pull toward the door I had come in through. "I'm kind of tired. Why don't we talk about it tomorrow?" I threw a thumb at the darkening skies outside. "It's close to sundown; been a long day, you know."

His hairless eyebrow scooted down his face. "It's four o'clock."

"Yeah," I said with an air of excuse-making. "But I nearly got strangled to death yesterday and it took a lot out of me. I'll stop by and talk with you tomorrow."

I threw a look at Zack, and I could tell he knew I was lying. "I can show you to the cafeteria if you want. You should probably eat before you sleep."

"Nah." I waved him off. "I'm just going to head back to the dorm. Thanks, though."

He froze next to the doctor, who was still squinting at me. "All right. See you around."

I gave them both a last wave and pushed my way out the door. I didn't run across the campus, but I definitely walked faster than normal. I wasn't used to the cold wind that whipped over the grounds as sundown approached. It felt like it was cutting right through me.

I walked into my dorm room and flipped on the lights. It

wasn't huge, but bigger than I would have expected. It had a full bathroom, a queen sized bed, small refrigerator, a desk and a walk-in closet. Some thoughtful person had even left a pen and paper on the stand next to the bed, in case I wanted to write a letter home to no one.

I checked the fridge and found a half dozen bottled waters. I pulled one out, broke the seal on it and dumped it down the sink in the bathroom. I washed out and refilled the water bottle from the tap. Can't be too careful.

I took a sip of water as I looked around the room. I didn't know much about video surveillance, but there were a half-dozen places they could have put a camera. The good news is that it was on the ground floor and there were big windows, so if they came for me in the middle of the night I could send a chair out the glass and follow behind. I had a reasonable amount of confidence that I could run faster than any of them. Hopefully fast enough to escape into the trees if need be.

I sat down on the bed and realized for the first time just how tense I was. My shoulder muscles were crying out for relief; I'd been walking around ready for someone (Wolfe) to come jumping out at me. I rubbed my neck with one hand while I held the bottle with the other.

The bedspread was dark navy, the only splash of color in a room that was a dim beige. It was so generic and stark, totally lacking in décor, it had to have been done by a guy. No woman could abide anything this plain and boring. I thought about how straightforward and businesslike Ariadne's wardrobe was and conceded that maybe she could have done it. But no one with any taste.

I found it hard to believe how much things had changed for me in the last couple days. My mind went once more to Reed, and I found myself wondering if he was okay. I thought about those brown eyes, and they hung in front of me. I lay back on the bed and they still lingered; and a few moments after I lay my head on the pillow, I fell into a deep sleep.

Seven

I knew I was dreaming. It was weird, but I could feel it, the darkness of the room just fading away as I slipped off to unconsciousness. Streaks of light from outside the window shot through my field of vision and a sensation of falling was replaced with a feeling of weightlessness, like the moment before you step down a stair in a dream and your heart catches and you wake.

Except I didn't wake. I saw Reed again, those brown eyes staring, searching for me. The haze around me began to lighten. Splashes of color entered the world around me and I realized Reed was coming into focus, details adding in front of my eyes. He looked at me with confusion. "Sienna? Where are we?"

I felt a chill and looked down. There were two figures at my feet. A face stared back at me with dead eyes. "I think we're in the parking lot of the grocery store where Wolfe found us."

He looked at me with practiced skepticism. "What's going on here?"

I shrugged. "I don't know."

He looked at the body at my feet. "I remember going to sleep…but this isn't like any dream I've ever had. In a dream, you can't pick your words, and ridiculous things happen. Like a man with a platter of cheese slices comes wandering through, and it seems totally normal until you wake up." He eyed me with an air of uncertainty. "Right?"

"I've never dreamed about a man with cheese slices."

"But you know what I mean? This really happened, right?" He looked down at the body. "I remember this guy's face."

Remembering the two men who died here – trying to help

me – took the thought of laughter away. "What happened to you? I woke up at the headquarters for those two clowns who broke into my house."

Reed flinched. "Yeah, I saw them get you. I had to bail. Wolfe messed me up pretty bad or I might have tried to fight them off."

I narrowed my eyes as I looked at him. "Are you a meta too?"

His hands fell to his waist. "Yeah."

"So what can you do? What's your...power?"

"The basics. Stronger than most. Nothing compared to that Wolfe guy, but I can tip over a car if I have to. I heal fast, of course. Some other stuff. Nothing major." He looked down, eyes avoiding mine.

"Uh huh. So why didn't you square with me when we were talking in the store?"

"It's your first day out in the world, you're running to escape from some guys who are shooting at you, and I get to break the news to you that you're a superhuman. Yeah," he said with sarcasm, "that wouldn't have sent you running away from me."

"It might not have." I thought about it for a minute. "Yeah, it probably would have before I met Wolfe. Where are you now?"

He shied away from my look again. "You're at their base?" He hesitated. "With those guys...from..."

"The Directorate. It's what they call themselves."

"Yeah. You're with them?"

"Not 'with them' like we're on the same team, but yeah. They want to run tests on me. Tell me what I am. Where are you?"

"Can't tell you." He cringed as he said it. "Sorry. I don't trust them."

I looked at him in annoyance. "I'm not staying here forever. I'm trying to decide if I want to let them figure things out for me before I leave. How am I supposed to find you if you won't tell me where you are?"

He finally looked me in the eye. "Seems like you've found a way to contact me. So talk to me again when you've escaped."

I threw my hands in the air. "Where am I supposed to go?"

He started to fade, getting hazy again, like there were gaps in his skin replaced by darkness. "Anywhere. Just get away from them."

I woke up with a start.

Eight

I sat up in bed and looked around. I hadn't even bothered to crawl under the covers. The red face of the digital clock on the dresser told me it was after midnight. I reached over and found the bottle of water I filled earlier. I picked it up, took it to the bathroom and dumped it out again. Just in case they snuck in while I was sleeping. Paranoia, thy name is Sienna.

After I filled it from the tap and drank two bottles, I laid back down on the bed. I was almost positive I had just talked to Reed in a dream. I went to sleep thinking of him and I dreamed of him. But he was right. What happened there was not like a regular dream. All the weirdness and surreal atmosphere of a dream was gone; it felt like we'd had a conversation in the waking world, but with a hazy backdrop.

Could I touch people's dreams? Was I a telepath, a mind reader? My thoughts raced while I thought about the possibilities. I'd never read a mind, so it probably wasn't that; unless it hadn't fully manifested as a power yet. Or maybe it was just limited to dreaming.

I thought about Mom as I lay there. Thought about when she used to get home, and how we'd eat dinner and talk about...I dunno, whatever. Training, mostly. TV shows, sometimes.

The world outside? Never. Rule #5. We don't talk about the outside world. It doesn't exist, for conversational purposes. We stay inside the house. The four walls that defined my life.

I thought about Mom and her rules and I wondered if maybe I could dream and talk to her, see where she was. I set the water bottle aside and lay back, this time crawling beneath the covers. I thought about her, about the smell of the chicken soup she used to heat up out of the can with the TV going in the background as we sat on the couch and talked. I recalled watching her walk out the door in the morning, and hoping that she'd open the outside door to the porch before the inside door to the house had shut, so I could catch just a glimpse of the outside world (she never did).

Then I thought of the times I'd disobeyed her. The times I'd let her down. I shuddered. The times she punished me.

The last time.

Somewhere in that succession of thoughts I drifted off again, and I woke to the sound of distant voices and a raging hunger. I blinked the bleariness out of my eyes and felt my skin covered in a cold sweat. My dreams this time had definitely not brought me to Mom. Light streamed in from a gray sky outside, peeking in through the blinds.

I padded into the bathroom and stripped off my clothing, which was sticking to my body. I thought for a moment about the idea of the Directorate watching me and I sighed, a deep, uncaring sound as I looked around the bathroom. I felt truly disgusting; there was still residual mud and grit in my hair from the parking lot two days ago when Wolfe had dropped me, even though someone had tried to clean it.

I sighed again and with a shrug I decided that I wanted a shower more than I wanted to worry about someone spying on me in the bathroom.

The hot water felt great, renewing me as it washed over my skin. Little flecks of dried blood that had caught in my sweater from the fight with Wolfe flaked off and swirled down the drain. I stayed in there longer than was necessary to get clean; the shower has long been my place for rejuvenation, the only spot where I could get privacy from Mom. The only place I'm allowed to shed my gloves, my shirt and all else.

I stepped onto the rug and took a moment to appreciate the

warmth of the dormitory bathroom. Even in a house as buttoned up as ours had been, drafts ran through it with alarming regularity. I could always tell what season it was by how cold I was when I got out of the shower. The bathroom here was perfectly insulated, though, and as I felt the soft squish of the plush bathmat between my toes there was a touch of that feeling of unfamiliarity again. It was as though I were so far outside my comfortable life that I almost couldn't recognize the actions I was taking as my own; like they were those of a stranger I was watching on TV.

I stepped out into my room wearing a towel and pulled open the closet to find a half dozen outfits. I took a look at the clothes I had discarded – dirty, disgusting and a little bloody. I wanted to put them back on, but it would undo the shower. Instead I picked out a black turtleneck and a pair of jeans and put them on, unsurprised to find that they fit me perfectly. I was only going to the cafeteria, but I grabbed the coat I had worn yesterday and slipped on my gloves, the only part of my ensemble not completely caked with filth. Rule #4. Old habits die hard.

The dormitory building was large and seemed to contain quite a few people. I guessed they were all metas like me, retrieved at some point or another by the Directorate. They seemed to be keeping to themselves, didn't meet my eyes in the corridors, which caused concern for me. Some of them hung together in small groups, and I could feel them looking when my back was turned.

I remembered seeing a sign for the cafeteria somewhere near the entrance I had used yesterday, so I walked the corridors looking for it. When I found one, I followed it to a large, open space with a hundred or more tables. Glass windows stretched from floor to ceiling of a two story-high space, looking out onto the snowy grounds. One wall opened up into a long serving line with a variety of different foods sitting out in a self-serve style, from Jell-O to meatloaf. A digital clock hung overhead, announcing that it was almost noon.

I passed through the line without difficulty; there was no cash register at the end, so I just walked off through the ever-increasing crowd and found a table by myself next to the window and sat down, ready to eat.

I was attacking the meatloaf when Ariadne sat down across from me. She wore an overly friendly look that put me on an annoyed footing made worse by some of my food choices. The coffee was not going well with the meatloaf. How was I supposed to know that? Mom never let me have coffee and people on TV drank it with everything. Bleh. Meatloaf tasted different than I expected, too.

Ariadne must have sensed my disquiet because I did not acknowledge her after she sat down. "Good morning," she said, breaking the silence. "Actually," she continued, smile widening, "I suppose I should say—"

"If the next words out of your mouth are 'Good afternoon,' I promise it won't be for you."

She blinked in slight shock. "Didn't—"

"Sleep well? No." My eyes narrowed as I lied. "Something about the thought of having a load of tests run didn't sit well with me."

"Does that mean you've decided against the testing?" Did I detect a note of disappointment in her voice?

"Didn't say that. I haven't decided yet. Either way, I'm not enthused about them."

"Ah." She nodded. "Perhaps we can help change your opinion. I've been asked to bring you to see the Director."

"Erich Winter?"

"Yes."

"Great." I slid aside the tray with the coffee and gawdawful meatloaf. "I'd like to ask him some questions anyway. Shall we?"

The priceless look of uncertainty on her face gave way to a

forced confidence as she led me downstairs to an underground tunnel leading to the headquarters building a few hundred yards away. "No need to walk through the snow if we don't have to," she said. I had wondered why she wasn't wearing a coat. She wore instead another colorless business suit, not the same as the one she'd had on when I met her but not different enough for me to care.

We emerged from the tunnel into the basement of the headquarters building and climbed a staircase to the fourth floor. I looked out the window as we walked down the corridor. The sky was still covered in clouds. I sighed. I had yet to see the sun.

We paused before a set of heavy wooden double doors. Ariadne knocked so softly I wondered if it was even possible to hear it inside. There was no answer but a moment later a click came from the handle and the door swung open to admit us. Ariadne gestured for me to go first but I shook my head and pointed for her to enter. She shrugged and did. I followed her a moment later.

The office was big, with a heavy stone desk standing in the middle of the room. It looked like a slab of flat rock that someone had propped up on two supporting blocks and used as a table, and it stretched about six feet across. There was no sign of paper on it anywhere, just a tablet computer. A lone painting of a winter landscape hung from the wall on the left hand side and two chairs were set before the desk for audiences.

Old Man Winter had opened the door, but by the time I was inside he'd already returned to his chair and sat down. He was tall, probably at least six foot five. His hair was close cropped on the sides and deep furrows were carved in the lines of his brow. His face was long, his eyes were sunken; bags hung beneath them, giving him a look of a man well over sixty and possibly over seventy. He was not thin but neither was he fat – he had a look of muscle and power that belied his years.

And his eyes were an icy, icy blue, and fixed with a stare that sent a deep chill through me.

"This is Sienna," Ariadne said to him, as though I could be anyone else. The only sign that he heard her was a slow, short nod, during which he never broke eye contact with me. I stared back, unwilling to be the first to look away. This was a game, I thought.

Ariadne said nothing and neither did he. He didn't blink, didn't look away, until finally my eyes were burning and I had to close them. He did not smile when I looked at him again, but I caught the thinnest suggestion of upward movement on his lips.

"Sienna is still considering whether or not to go through with the testing," Ariadne informed him. He sat stock still in his chair behind the desk and continued to stare me down. I like to think a lesser person would be intimidated by his constant eye contact. I was annoyed. "She has questions for you."

His gray eyebrows rose as if he were asking a question of his own. He waved his hand at me in a vague gesture that I took as a sign to proceed with my inquiries.

I stared back at him, trying my utmost not to blink. "Do you know what happened to my mother?"

He shook his head slowly, breaking eye contact for the first time since I entered the room. "No." His voice carried an obvious Germanic accent, even in the brief response. He raised his hand toward me once more, indicating to ask my next question.

I tried my hardest not to glare, but I probably failed. "Who would know?"

This time the eyebrow rose only a hint and he glanced toward Ariadne, who answered for him. "We have a variety of different sources of gathering information, including sending some of our agents to question people under the guise of being police officers investigating her disappearance. I have a report that you can read, but here's the gist: your mother has been working as an MRI technician at Hennepin County Medical Center for the last fourteen years under an assumed name—"

"So she's really not Sierra Nealon?" I asked without surprise.

Ariadne's fake smile held more patience than irony. "She is. She's been working under the name Brittany Eccleston. She has friends and co-workers, a pretty well established life built around her work – and none of them that we questioned knew she had a daughter." Ariadne hesitated. "She's had a reasonably active social life, dinners with friends, though not much indication that she's done any dating—"

"Did she ever mention any men? Your father, for instance?" Old Man Winter spoke up, his voice at a low timbre, smooth and accented.

"No." I shrugged, indifferent. Mom didn't talk about men. It wasn't in the rules; it just never happened. "Why, are you my father?"

Amusement crossed his weathered features, but only for a moment. "Hardly."

I shrugged again. "Just curious. I heard you worked with my mom back in the old days and I have no idea who my dad is."

His head inclined in a nod. "I did not know her well. The agency was large and I was not in a position of influence."

"What did you do?"

His reply was a slight shrug, his large shoulders moving only a few centimeters, as if he were trying to conserve energy by making as little movement as possible.

"I think what's important," Ariadne reinserted herself into the conversation, "is that we help you find her. And if we can assist you along the way by answering questions about what kind of powers you have, that would be of interest to you, wouldn't it?"

I chuckled, more to myself than anyone. "I'll figure it out."

Ariadne's expression hardened. "Assuming you have the time. There's a pretty dangerous monster hunting you."

I looked back at Old Man Winter, and he was watching me,

gauging my reaction to the threat of Wolfe. "He's a real bastard," I replied, "but I'm not going to spend the rest of my life hiding out here on your campus, even if I did consent to your tests – which I haven't, yet."

Ariadne and Old Man Winter exchanged a look. Concern from her; obvious, easy to read. From him, harder to tell, but I thought I saw amusement again.

She turned back to me. "Let me be honest—"

"First time ever?" I cracked. "Give it a shot."

She ignored my jibe. "Your mother was powerful, but the records of her capabilities were lost in the destruction of the Agency. We have no idea who your father was, if he was a meta, what capabilities he might have had, but given your mother's likely exposure to metas in her work, we'd expect he probably was. Based on our observations of your healing abilities, your strength – yes, we saw you lift the bench, well done – we suspect you're quite powerful. We want to know—" she focused on me— "what you're capable of, and frankly, we'd like you to join us."

This time I let loose more than a chuckle. "Join you? Why?"

"We do important work here," she said, undeterred by my laugh. "Keeping the meta-human population from running amok while helping them to fully understand and control their abilities is a noble task."

"I'm not going to argue that you need to police these metas," I said. "But I haven't even come to a decision on the testing, so I doubt you're going to be getting much consideration on your offer until I have that one figured out."

She looked back at Old Man Winter one more time and he nodded again, one of those subtle blink-and-you-miss-it head motions. She turned back to me. "What do you want?"

I smiled, wide, with a joviality I really didn't feel. "I want to go home."

Nine

"Excuse me?" Ariadne stared back at me open-mouthed. "Did getting strangled cause you brain damage? Don't you think that your house would be the first place Wolfe would try to re-acquire you?"

"Re-acquire?" I scoffed. "He didn't acquire me in the first place."

She looked at me with something short of astonishment. "He damned near did – if it hadn't been for our agents showing up when they did—"

"No," I said with a vehement shake of my head. Old Man Winter hadn't shown the slightest reaction to our entire exchange. "By the time your boys showed up I had pumped Wolfe so full of tranquilizer darts he'd have had a hell of a time fighting off a grasshopper, let alone carry me away."

"Wolfe jumped a ten foot tall fence to escape from Kurt and Zack," she said, her jaw clenching. "Maybe you missed that too, since you were unconscious in a pool of your own blood when it happened."

I rolled my eyes. I am a teenager; might as well fight like a one. "I want to go home – not permanently, but I have some personal effects I'd like to retrieve." I turned an irritable gaze from Ariadne to Old Man Winter.

He stared back, still unblinking.

"No," Ariadne said. "You're far too valuable to risk Wolfe getting his hands on you. We have no idea who he works for, if he works for anybody – or what he wants with you, but it's nothing good."

"Ah ha!" I crowed. "So you *do* intend to keep me here against my will!"

"No," came the quiet, accented voice of Old Man Winter. "If you want things from your home, perhaps we can come to an agreement."

I looked at him. "I'm listening."

He turned to Ariadne, who spoke in his stead. "We send agents to retrieve whatever you want and bring it back here. In exchange, you do the tests."

I thought about it for a minute. "Counter-offer – and be assured, I'm not really offering so much as telling you what I'll accept. You send your agents to the house to confirm it's clear and I go in and get what I want and need, and we leave in five minutes or less. I do the testing after."

"Are you suicidal?" Ariadne looked at me in amazement. "You know Wolfe will be there somewhere, watching. At least if we're going to engage in this madness, let's wait until M-Squad returns—"

Old Man Winter cut her off, soft voice firm. "They will not be back for some time. We will send agents – ten should suffice to scout and keep a perimeter." He looked back to me. "Your terms are acceptable. Dr. Sessions will test you when you return."

"No cutting," I said to him, finding that this time his expression hinted at amusement, "nothing invasive, my hands will be free at all times, and don't expect me to drink anything."

He nodded once more and she bit back her response but shot him a look that indicated great displeasure. "Very well." With a curt nod of her head that reminded me of a bow of submission, she backed toward the door. I followed her and cast a last look at Old Man Winter before I left. He stared back, unapologetic, watching, surveying, who knew what for.

The door closed with a soft click and Ariadne rounded on me. I could tell by the fire in her eyes that she was preparing to unload. "Stick it," I told her. "Call me when your boys are ready to leave." I didn't bother to look back to see what reaction my words had caused. Well, maybe a little peek. Not sure why antagonizing her was so enjoyable; it wasn't like she'd done anything to wrong me.

I was sitting on my bed a few hours later when I heard a knock on the door. When I opened it, Zack was waiting with a dour look. "Ready to get killed?" His expression did not show any hint of lightness.

I smiled, trying to lighten his mood. "I thought you guys were going to sweep the house and the area first to make sure Wolfe isn't around?"

He gave me a kind of exasperated shrug with a marked exhalation. "Kurt and I get to sit in the car with you until we get the all-clear, but let's not fool ourselves. If Wolfe's strategy is to not be seen, he won't be seen – until it's too late. If his strategy is to take one of our guys and squeeze him until he lies and says it's all clear, then that's what he'll do and we still won't see him until it's too late." His eyes blazed. "Wolfe is the most dangerous meta I've heard of and it's insane that we're going into this without M-Squad for backup."

"Have you guys run across him before?"

"Nope," Zack said without emotion. "But one of our other branches did, and it ended bloody. Just like every other story in his file."

I scoffed. "He's not some invisible boogeyman. He has weaknesses, and he can't be everywhere at once. Maybe he's watching my house, maybe he's not." I stared him down as another possibility occurred to me. "Why couldn't he be here, watching the Directorate campus?"

Zack's hand crept up to his face, covering his eyes as he rubbed the bridge of his nose. "I don't know that he's not, but I know we stand a better chance of taking him here than in the middle of a South Minneapolis neighborhood. What could possibly be in your house that's so damned important that you're willing to risk your life and ours?"

I didn't answer him. He shook his head and gestured for me to follow him, which I did. The truth was, I didn't need anything from my house. When we got there, I was going to load up as many weapons as I could carry from the basement, but I didn't really need any of them. And it's not like any of my clothes were so amazing that I couldn't live without them; nor personal items, none of it.

I wanted to go back because I thought Wolfe would be there.

I hated the way I felt after our last fight, that sick feeling in the pit of my stomach thinking about it – about how he beat me down, made me fear him. I wanted to run into him. This time I'd be ready. Mobility and agility were my weapons. I couldn't beat him for strength, but I moved faster than him last time and if I hadn't rammed my head into the iron wall of muscle that was his stomach...I think I could take him. I wanted to. I was faster than him, I knew it. Not by much, but enough. I just had to aim for the weak points – eyes, groin, kidneys.

At least it would be better than sitting around the Directorate for tests I didn't really want to do, waiting for a mom who probably wasn't going to show up.

I followed Zack to an underground parking garage where I found ten guys, all dressed in suits, carrying rifles and shotguns. Kurt was standing there waiting and he greeted me with a scowl and a grunt that bordered on rude. I waved coquettishly with a big, fake smile. "I should get a gun too," I said as Zack and I walked up to their car.

"No," they both chorused. I shrugged; I hadn't expected them to say yes and I didn't press the point. If I was facing off against Wolfe and needed one, I'd take it from an agent. When Wolfe showed, I knew I was going to have to move fast; I didn't want any of these guys to die, after all.

We drove to a gate that opened for us, the entrance to the Directorate compound, which was surrounded by a high brick wall. I counted three security cameras without difficulty and I had a suspicion that those were for show; I would have bet the real cameras were much smaller.

We drove down straight roads in a convoy, empty fields of rolling hills on either side. After about twenty minutes we hit a major highway and followed it for another twenty minutes until we hit a suburban area replete with malls, stores and retail outlets. Another few minutes and we exited a freeway into an area of older homes that looked familiar. I couldn't be sure, but I thought it was the same cross street where Reed and I entered the freeway a couple days before.

A few streets later I found myself staring at the front of a house that should have looked familiar, since I lived in it, but didn't because I hadn't seen the exterior in over a decade except while fleeing from it in a rush.

"We'll wait here until we get the all-clear," Zack told me, leaning over the seat to talk to me. A few of the cars parked in front of us emptied and the agents were all wearing full length coats to conceal their weapons. They streamed across the street in a mass.

"Um," I said with amusement, "shouldn't we have parked a few streets away if we're afraid Wolfe is watching the house?"

"Wow, you've outsmarted us. It must be our first day on the job," Kurt answered with a snotty air of aggravation. "We are a few streets away. They're going to walk the three blocks to get to your place."

I looked at the house I had thought was mine. I tried to reconcile the facade with the brief glimpse I had gotten of my home as I fled into Reed's car days earlier. I shook my head. They were all snow covered, blotting out differences between them. I gave up and looked at Zack, who was shaking his head at his partner.

We sat in silence for the next few minutes. Tempted as I was to make smartass comments to annoy Kurt to the point where he'd get out of the car, I restrained myself (not sure how). We waited, tension filling the air as mundane reports from the agents came across their radios. Staticky "all clear" calls came through over and over. Zack had unplugged his microphone so it piped out over a speaker.

I gnawed on one of my fingernails as I listened. The voices didn't sound unhappy, just clipped and professional. I wondered if Wolfe would show up, if he was even looking for me here. I mean, he couldn't just hang around my house all day, every day waiting for me to show up, could he?

I thought about those black, soulless eyes and suppressed a shudder. He could. He would. I had to act fast here, get to him before he got to anybody else. My ears focused on the radio, waiting for the first hint of any trouble.

"Found something in the basement," came the voice over the speaker. I felt myself tense. If it wasn't Wolfe, I could bet I knew what they found. "It's…ugh…well, it's not Wolfe. All clear."

"All clear," came another voice in agreement. "That's the whole house."

"You haven't sent anybody here since the day I left?" I asked Zack, who was staring into space, concentrating.

"No." His head gave a quick shake. "You ready?"

"Yeah," I replied. "Is our driver going to give us curbside service or do we have to walk from here?" I looked at Kurt and the flash of a scowl was my reward.

"One of these days, little Miss Daisy, you and I are going to go head to head," he growled as he threw the car in gear and stomped on the accelerator.

"And I shall look forward to that day with greatest

anticipation," I said in a mocking southern accent, "if for no other reason than I'll get to watch your head cave in from finally meeting one stronger."

He said nothing else as we turned and flew down an alley, almost taking out a garbage can. His next turn was almost as violent and I didn't get a chance to ask whether he was scared and pissed or just a bad driver, because he came to a screeching halt and the wheel hit the curb.

"Settle down," Zack told him, wide-eyed.

"I'll settle down when we're out of here."

"Only if you can find a nice fella who'll take you," I quipped.

"Oh, how quaint, a gay joke," Kurt said without turning back. "I'm married."

"Actually it was my way of calling you a little girl. What's his name?"

"Haha. To a woman."

"Shocking! Because no reasonable man would have you?"

"Can it, please." Zack turned to me. "We're here. Let's hurry and get the hell out."

"Sure," I said as I slid over and opened the door, stepping out onto the curb covered in a half foot of snow. He parked this way intentionally. Ass. "Just trying to express my happiness for your pissy partner that he could find someone to put up with his menstrual cycles." That wicked feeling of glee buoyed itself in my soul again as I stepped onto the sidewalk. I ignored Kurt, who made a rude gesture at me from behind the trunk and made no move to join us.

Zack followed me up the driveway, which had a thin layer of snow over it. I wondered if Mom used to shovel it herself after a snowstorm? No...she was always dressed nice before she went to work. Flurries fell around me and I found myself sticking out my tongue, trying to catch one.

Zack watched me with a small smile of amusement that evaporated after a few seconds. "We're in a hurry, remember?"

My goofy grin faded. "Right."

There was an agent at the door of the porch, hands buried inside his coat. I stepped past him with a sarcastic salute and he rolled his eyes and smiled. Now there was a man with a sense of humor. The screens and windows of the porch were all boarded up and covered – so that when Mom left in the morning, I couldn't see outside.

It was dark as we stepped into the entry. The lights were on, but they didn't cast much light compared to even the cloudy sky outside. I looked around the living room. Everything was where we left it, upturned furniture and all. There were a few darts sticking out of the walls, and a couple of the agents were chuckling over them.

I smiled as I passed them and brushed into my room. A few articles of clothing were on the bed, not where I left them, since the last thing I did before I left was sleep and then whoop the hell out of Zack and Kurt.

I felt Zack edge up behind me. "If your men didn't move these clothes around, someone else has been here," I told him.

He had the radio plugged back in and I saw his fingers move to touch his ear. "Did anyone move any clothes in this room?" He paused for a moment, waiting for responses, then looked back at me and shook his head. "Guess he's been here."

"Or someone has," I replied.

He handed me a black duffel bag that he'd had slung over his shoulder. "Get what you came for and let's go."

I threw some clothes in the bag at random, then tossed in my eskrima sticks after retrieving them from where I left them behind the couch in the living room. As I picked them up I half-smiled, half-frowned as I remembered leaving them behind while I crawled away from Kurt as he fired his dart gun at me.

"Is that it?" Zack's voice almost cracked with the sound of his nerves. "Can we go yet?"

"Just a few more things," I said as I headed toward the door to the basement. My hand froze for a moment at the handle, then I slowly turned it. "Anyone down there?" I asked as I hovered in the doorjamb, waiting for Zack's answer.

He shot a look at the other agents in the room. "Not right now."

The white plaster of the living room walls gave way to concrete block at the entry to the basement. The staircase made an abrupt turn to the left ahead, following the foundation of the house. The steps were an old, unvarnished wood, and the only illumination was the single light overhead. I used to walk down these steps several times per day, but it was the last time I came up them that was giving me pause.

I reached the landing and turned, most of my thoughts about Wolfe forgotten. I knew he wasn't down here. The smell of old sweat, blood and other foulness filled the air.

I looked back at Zack and saw him scrunch his nose in displeasure at the aroma. "Did your mother kill someone down here?"

I didn't blink. "No. But not for lack of trying."

He laughed, and I continued down the last few steps and felt the concrete underfoot. Even though there was a thick sole on the boots I was wearing, my mind filled in the sensation from the thousands of times I had trod these floors barefoot while Mom was away, giving my feet a ghostly feel of the familiar chill. It crept up my legs, infusing my body, and I felt an involuntary tremor run through me.

The smell was worse down here, and my eyes wandered over our assorted weapons, hanging from hooks on the far wall. Katanas, nunchuks, scythe, rapiers and so many more. Mats covered the floors in the middle of the room and pipes crisscrossed the ceiling overhead from the exposed beams of the floor above. A slight clinking could be heard from overhead, as well as soft footsteps of the agents treading upstairs.

A couple of buried windows provided a little bit of light in the back, but they were covered by a film of white, providing enough opacity that it was impossible to distinguish anything through them. For illumination there were three naked bulbs swinging from the ceiling. In the far corner I could see the faint outline of a blocky shape in the shadows and the tremor got a little worse; I shook for a second.

I had halted in place and I felt Zack's hand brush my shoulder. I looked back in slight surprise and found his eyes looking into mine. My goodness, they were pretty. "Hurry up, okay?" His face was all sincerity, so I shook off my reverie and pushed myself to cross the mats to the far wall. I pulled a katana off the hooks and slid it into the loops of the bag, then threw a pair of sais and a dagger into it as well.

Zack watched me with wide eyes and a look of abject absurdity. "If you wanted weapons, we had plenty back at the Directorate…"

"Just figured I'd get them while I'm here," I replied. "Besides, Kurt's not too keen on me being armed."

"I'm not that excited about it either," he admitted with a wry grin. "But that's because I've felt what you can do with those sticks."

"In fairness, you did break into my house."

"Yeah, I…" His words trailed off as he looked into the corner. "What is that?" He started across the mats to join me on the far wall, but I met him halfway.

"Nothing. I'm done, we can go."

"No, wait." He was peering into the darkness.

"It's really nothing. You were worried about Wolfe, weren't you?" I plastered a smile on my face. "We should go."

"Just a minute." He reached up and grasped one of the overhead lights, pointing it toward the corner. He took a step closer and I withheld any additional protests and felt myself brace internally. I turned away and shut my eyes, facing the stairs and took a couple steps in that direction. There was an agonizing and sudden tightness in my belly. "What…is…this?" Zack's voice was low, but rising with each syllable, incredulous. I heard the squeak of hinges behind me, then retching from Zack, then a firm declaration. "Oh my God. Oh my God."

I squeezed my eyes shut tighter.

"OH. MY. GOD!" The last declaration was the most frightening, but it was nothing compared to the sound that followed it.

"I'm not a god, but it's always nice to get a compliment." I opened my eyes to find twin pools of blackness staring into mine from just a few feet away as he descended the stairwell. "Hello, little doll," Wolfe breathed. "Time to play."

Ten

"Hello, big poodle," I replied, edge in my voice. "Time for your ass to get housebroken." My hand had been clutching the katana and it slid from its scabbard, all thoughts of Zack's discovery filed away to be dealt with later. I whipped the blade across Wolfe's chest as he dodged, fast as I remembered.

Unfortunately for him, he dodged into the bag I threw with my outstretched hand. He recoiled when it hit, making me believe that one of the eskrima sticks got a piece of his face. Not enough to do any damage, but enough to piss him off. He grabbed the strap as it fell and winged it back at me with a little extra mustard. I dodged as it flew by, katana in my hands and a self-satisfied smile on my lips.

"You're awfully confident," Wolfe said as he slid sideways in a feint, "considering last time we met I left you broken on the pavement."

"It was two days ago," I cooed, "and I'm all better, so I don't think you broke me."

"She likes it rough," he said with enough suggestion that I doubly wanted to chop him into ground beef.

"Last time we met," Zack said from Wolfe's side, shotgun in his hand, raising it toward the beastly, hairy face, "I ran your canine ass off, in case you forgot."

"Wolfe doesn't forget," the beast said with a smile. "He was feeling a bit out of sorts and couldn't play; otherwise he would have enjoyed eating your entrails." Wolfe cocked his hand back and flung it at Zack faster than the agent could dodge. The hit blasted the young man in the face and the crunch told me something broke – either the cartilage in his nose or a bone in his cheek – and the Directorate agent crumpled to the ground. But not before the shotgun discharged into Wolfe's side, leaving holes in his already dirty shirt. No blood trickled out.

I met Wolfe's eyes as he lunged for me. I evaded and clipped him with my sword, ripping his shirt further. He didn't even finish his landing before he reached for me again. His arms were long but my sword was longer and it dragged across his wrist as I dodged him again.

I looked at the place where the blade had kissed him but there was no evident sign of contact; only immaculate skin with twisted black hairs all over it. He caught me looking and made a very predatorial tsk-tsk sound. "Wolfe has very thick skin, little doll. Bullets don't hurt him much." He reached down and lifted his shirt where the shotgun blast had impacted. It was very hairy, but the only things visible were small red discolorations – not even a break in the skin.

My mind reeled. *He's not vulnerable to the shotgun*, I thought. *Maybe a pistol or a rifle – if I had one*. Desperation filled me. *My sword doesn't seem to do much in glancing blows – but maybe a full on, impaling strike...but doing that would put me in reach of his arms, unless I did it from behind...*

I was faster than him, I reflected as he jumped for me and I dodged him again. Every time he lunged he had to commit all his momentum to his forward motion, and when he missed he was off balance for just a second. I slipped to his right on his next lunge and drove my sword down with all my strength, aiming at his Achilles tendon at the back of his leg. My sword blade sliced through his baggy, dirty pants and caught him right above the heel.

I felt the blade stop against my gloves as though I had driven the sword into a steel block. A grunt from Wolfe was all the acknowledgment I got for my efforts and I rolled to my right as he turned and I narrowly dodged a wild swing from him.

"Little doll," he growled, the menace in his voice sending chills through me, "Wolfe's amusement is running low…Wolfe is bleeding…and Wolfe doesn't like bleeding…a few drops of his blood is of more worth than this entire, stinking gutter trash city…"

I chanced to look down at my handiwork on his ankle, but what was there could scarcely be described as bleeding. A few drops no bigger than the head of a pin dotted the mat where he was standing. His grin had faded, replaced by a look of savagery that brought back the fear of our first encounter full force. I was face to face with a seemingly unkillable menace – what was I supposed to do now? Run for the stairs? He'd catch me on the turn.

My breathing had become ragged, not from exertion but from fear. I put myself in this situation because I was sure I could beat him. Now I was almost sure I couldn't. Unless…

I lunged forward before he made another move, holding my sword at maximum extension and aiming for his eye. I might not be able to break his skin, but the eyes were always a weak point…

Once more I felt the blade stop as though it hit an immovable object. I opened my eyes (I hadn't realized I closed them when I lunged – Mother would have been very upset with me) and saw his hand wrapped around my katana, the tip stopped only inches from his right eye. I pushed it harder, and watched as a thin trickle of red ran down his wrist. He yanked the blade down to his chest level and pulled it toward him. I let it go, but not before he had pulled me off balance and brought me within his reach.

This close to him, I had a revelation. Where a normal person would have fingernails, he had claws. They jutted out an inch or so above the ends of his fingers, black, with a pointed tip that looked sharp. They seemed to extend as I watched them.

I tried to stagger back but he seized my right arm and his claws raked into the skin, shredding through my sleeve. I pulled away and fell down, rolling to my feet and slipping away just in time to avoid a slash. I felt my back bump into the wall and realized he had cornered me. I reached up by instinct and grabbed for a weapon, pulling down a dagger and holding it in front of me as he leaped forward and slammed into me, driving me into the wall.

I opened my eyes and I felt like I'd lost a few seconds. My head spun from the impact. Wolfe was big; I would have bet he weighed well over three hundred pounds. I took a sharp intake of breath and realized he had been laying across me; that he had actually broken through the concrete block of the basement wall by driving my body into it. The powdered dust from the destruction hung in the air like a haze over me as I lolled in some twilight form of consciousness.

I tried to move my arms but failed. There was a long shadow stretching to the ceiling above me and it reached down with a pointed hand and grasped me, once more, around the neck, hauling me into the air. I knew my feet were dangling below me, but I couldn't feel them. I looked into those black eyes and my view expanded a little, like a camera when it zooms out, and I realized his face was contorted with rage.

"Look what you did to Wolfe, little doll." He shook me, hanging in the air as I was, and twisted my neck so that my eyes rolled toward his midsection. The knife I had pulled from the wall and stuck out to stop him was buried in his gut and a steady stream of blood had soaked his shirt. I would have smiled, but I wasn't really in a position to.

His hand wasn't choking me this time, just dangling me in place. I realized later that I must have been concussed when he smashed me through the wall; had some bones broken, probably my spine as well, because the feeling in my extremities was missing.

"Wolfe is tired of the way you play." He pulled me closer to him and I felt his nose run along my neck, heard the faint sound of sniffing. "I don't think you can move now…" The ominous way he said it turned my stomach. "Now Wolfe can play with you his way…without any interruptions—"

Before I could find out what that meant (though I had a disgusting theory) a flash of light seared my eyes and something rocked Wolfe from behind. He dropped me and I fell to my side, curled up. Upon impact, I lay there for a moment, unmoving, then realized I could now feel my arms, my legs and everything else. And they all hurt. Another flash of light lit the room and I sat up, nursing a half dozen cuts and some agonizing pain in my back and neck.

Kurt Hannegan stood at the bottom of the stairs, eyes blazing, what was left of his hair in disarray. In his hands was a shining silver gun unlike any I'd seen before, with a series of three cylindrical barrels that were smoking. "Can you move?"

I nodded, blanching from the pain that filled me.

"Then go!" He jerked a thumb toward the stairs as he pointed the weapon at Wolfe once more and fired. The barrels emitted a beam of pure white and Wolfe's body shook, pushing him from his side to his back. His nose twitched and his eyes, though glossy, looked at me with inarticulate rage. His hand slid from where it lay to grasp me around the ankle, just barely holding it.

"Little doll…"

I ripped my ankle from his grasp and brought it down hard on his face. Then again. When I lifted my foot, I saw him smiling. He tried to roll to his side but failed.

"GET MOVING!" Hannegan fired twice in rapid succession, his blasts rolling Wolfe to a facedown position.

I staggered over to Zack, whose eyes were shut, his face a bloody mess. "We have to get him out of here," I said to Kurt.

"Dammit," I heard Hannegan mutter under his breath. The gun went off twice more when my back was turned and I shot a look back to Wolfe, who was fighting to get back to his feet. "I'm running out of juice for this thing!"

I reached down to Zack and wrapped an arm under his chest and pulled. Lifting him was only marginally more difficult than walking by myself was at this point. Unfortunately, walking by myself was quite the challenge. I made for the staircase, supporting him as I climbed. I heard the gun discharge twice more, then some swearing from Kurt, and heavy footfalls on the stairs behind me as I turned the corner and entered the living room.

I staggered past the sofa, pausing for a beat as I saw two dead Directorate agents in the living room, one with a look of shock on his face, the other missing his head. I stepped over another body on the porch, this one missing at least one arm. Another was splayed out under the tree in the front yard as though he were napping in the snow. I almost slipped at the same spot as last time I left the house, but recovered.

I opened the door to the backseat and threw Zack in, then hobbled to the front just as Kurt cleared the driveway. He slid into the driver's seat and was already starting the car as he slammed the door. His foot was on the accelerator before it was in gear, causing a loud thump as the car rocked and the tires slipped on the snowy pavement.

I looked back at the house. Wolfe staggered out the front door, clutching his ribs, and broke into a run as we shot down the street.

"He's gaining on us!" I shouted as I looked back, watching Wolfe streak along behind us, loping on all fours. Like a dog.

Kurt took the corner so fast we slid until the wheels caught and took off again. I heard a screeching noise and turned to see Wolfe dig his claws into the trunk. Little bits of metal flaked off as if they were paper. I looked through the rear window and saw those black eyes staring back at me, the mouth of the demon upturned in a grin. I couldn't take my eyes off him. He was keeping pace with the car, barely, trying to use his claws to secure a hold to grab on.

Kurt floored it as we shot through another intersection, then turned to get on the freeway. Wolfe's hands fell free of the trunk, but he kept running behind us, still watching me. He maintained his pace all the way to the top of the onramp, at which point Kurt put the accelerator to the floor and I saw Wolfe's black eyes recede in the distance as we made our escape.

Eleven

As the car sped down the interstate, I stole a look at the speedometer. Kurt was doing close to a hundred as I slipped into the back seat and knelt on the floorboard next to Zack. One of my gloved hands held his head while the other wiped the blood from his face. It flowed from his nose, which was broken. The rest of his handsome face seemed unharmed and his eyes fluttered open.

"What happened?" he asked, woozy.

"Wolfe," I replied.

"Oh. Did we win?"

I heard a snort from Kurt in the front seat. "Do you feel like you won, kid?"

He turned his face to look at the back of Kurt's head. "I'm still alive, so yeah. Kinda." His hand crept up to his nose and held it, stemming the bleeding. He sat up, his eyeballs rolling. "What about the other guys?" He looked at Kurt, who made no move but to stiffen and keep focused on the road.

Zack turned to me. His eyes met mine and I had to look away. "I don't think there were any survivors," I said, looking down.

"How did we get away?" His voice carried a dreamlike quality.

Kurt harrumphed in the front seat. I shot a glare at him. "Your partner shot Wolfe with some kind of epic blaster weapon that kept him down while I carried you out. Why weren't all your guys carrying those?"

Kurt didn't deign to look back. "Because that's the only one we had."

I looked back to see Zack studying me. "You're hurt," he said.

"You too."

"Lean forward." He gently pushed me toward the front seat. "Your shirt is bloody in the back."

He started to lift my sweater but my hand brushed his away. "I'm fine," I assured him. "Wolfe rammed me into the wall but I'm already healing."

"I should check." Concern lit his slender face and warm eyes. I stared a moment too long, got embarrassed and looked away again. Damn.

I ran my gloved hand down my back and felt a half dozen places where it hurt, but wasn't agonizing. Then my hands moved to my front and I found some broken ribs and cringed. "I'm fine," I said as he started to lean toward me. "Really. I'll be back to a hundred percent before you know it."

"Must be nice," Kurt spat. "I know a few guys that wish they had that ability right now."

"Kurt…" Zack started.

"What?" Kurt's tone was acid in reply, and he shot a look of pure malice at me. "Miss High And Mighty Little Meta got them killed. Is that too deep for you, Zack? Are you too busy staring into her eyes to realize that there are eight of our guys dead because of her?"

"Shut up!" Zack answered for me, but I was smoldering on the inside. I couldn't deny the truth of what he was saying, but it didn't make it sting any less. They were dead because of me.

"We didn't walk out of there with whatever it was she went for," Kurt went on, voice breaking like a man on the edge. "What did you need to get from your house that was SO important, little girl, that you'd risk meeting up with Wolfe to get it?"

I opened my mouth to speak but no words came out. I stuttered for a minute before Kurt cut me off.

"I see. Well, I'm glad it was so important that it was worth all those men's lives. Some of them have families, you know—"

"Enough." Zack's voice was commanding enough that Kurt stopped, leaving a pall hanging in the air between the three of us that Zack broke as he leaned in close to me. "In the basement, what I found…"

"I don't want to talk about that now." I lowered my voice. "Not with *him* here."

"But you'll talk about it later?" I felt pinned down by his gaze.

"Yes."

"All right." He nodded. "But what were you after? Why did we go back?"

"Later." I tried to put enough emphasis into my words that he'd stop, and he did. We rode in silence.

The drive back seemed to take forever, the cityscape fading into country lanes, and after an eternity on the road we were motioned through the gate onto the campus of the Directorate. Kurt had talked on his cell phone, and I got the feeling from his side of the conversation that we had a meeting to attend as soon as we returned.

That thought was confirmed when we pulled into the garage under the headquarters building. Ariadne waited for us, her blasé suit blending in to the dim light of the motor pool. She exchanged a perfunctory greeting with Zack and Kurt that was less warm than the relieved one she greeted me with, and then she led us to an elevator that went straight to the top floor. We followed her to the double doors leading to Old Man Winter's office.

He was sitting in his chair when Ariadne brought us in. He made no move to offer seats, but Kurt took one and Zack gestured for me to take the other. Ariadne walked past Old Man Winter and stood behind him, facing the window, showing the entire room her skinny ass.

Sorry, that was probably me projecting some anger.

"Wolfe?" Old Man Winter's thick eyebrows moved almost unnaturally, but it was the only sign of motion on his face other than some faint curling on his lips as he spoke.

"Still alive," Kurt replied. "I hit him with the cannon until the charge was out, but it didn't have a lot of effect."

Old Man Winter's eyes moved to Zack, who hesitated. "I think he knocked me out before I got a shot off, sir."

"No," I said before Old Man Winter could reply, shifting his penetrating gaze back to me, "Zack hit him in the side point blank with a shotgun blast. Wolfe showed me after it happened – all it did was leave a few red marks. His skin is thick; really resistant to blades, bullets and the like."

Old Man Winter surveyed us all. His shocking blue eyes made me uncomfortable as I waited for him to speak, to say something, anything. He didn't.

Ariadne did. "Yet somehow, last time—" she turned from the window and looked at me—"you managed to penetrate his skin with darts and drug him."

"Those dart guns were designed by Doc Sessions," Kurt interjected. "They have a microtip, smaller than any needle, so they inject without breaking the skin." He tossed a sneer at me. "It's nothing she did."

"Yeah, well, I hurt him this time, too," I said as I wiped some blood off my lips with my glove. I looked down; the dark drops blended well with the black leather, leaving it looking shiny and wet. "And I didn't need a portable howitzer to do it."

"Yeah, because you stuck out a dagger and let him run you through a wall." His face was red with anger, a flush that extended to the balding spots on his head. "I've got a great idea to stop him; let's stick you in front of him with a bigger sword and let him put you through a wall again – and again – until one of you dies. I know which one of you I'm rooting for—"

"At least I tried," I said, not looking up from my glove. "I didn't sit around in the corner waiting to die."

"Oho, courage from the meta-bitch," Kurt said, standing up. Zack stepped between us, unsteady on his feet, but I didn't budge from my chair. "Yeah, you got a lot of guts to back up the inhuman strength and super-fast healing. Why, I don't know how us normal folks that just break and die when Wolfe hits us can be so cowardly! Except we weren't, because a lot of good guys died today so that he could get another shot at you—"

"Maybe it was the other way around," I said, turning to meet his accusation. "Maybe I wanted another shot at him."

Everyone froze. Kurt looked down at me with an almost total lack of understanding. A look of knowing had dawned across Zack's face while Ariadne appeared stricken at the window. Old Man Winter, as per usual, kept his expression neutral through either long practice or a complete lack of emotional attachment to the situation. I suspected the former, but I didn't know him well enough to be sure.

It felt like the air had stagnated, as though everybody had paused and no one was taking any breaths; as though I had tossed out a grenade in the middle of the room and we were just waiting for it to explode.

"You did it on purpose." Kurt was the first to recover. "You didn't go back for anything; you went there so you could take a crack at Wolfe, and you threw away eight of our guys in the process, you—!" He lunged at me, screaming unintelligibly, and Zack caught him midway, struggling to control his partner's bulk as Kurt pushed toward me.

I continued to stare at the blood in my glove. It was a few drops; nothing compared to what was on my hands.

"Get him out of here, Davis!" Ariadne's shout crackled through the air. "Hannegan, get yourself under control!"

I turned to look at Kurt, whose face was purple with outrage.

Zack was no longer restraining him, but he still held a protective arm out between me and Kurt. I didn't need it. Beaten, wounded, internally bleeding and I could still have broken him into tiny pieces, then everyone else in the room one by one. Sweet gesture, though.

"Zack," Ariadne called out to him. "Go to medical. You look like Hannegan drove over you."

They walked out together, Kurt storming and Zack following a few paces behind. Zack turned back to meet my eyes at the door and mouthed the word "Later" before he closed it. If Kurt had said it, I would have considered it a weak threat. With Zack, I knew it was a promise – of a conversation that I didn't want to have. Ever. I sighed and turned back to Ariadne and Old Man Winter.

Ariadne seemed to be struggling for words and I recalled our last conversation and my suggestive insult. "We are…glad to see you made it through this episode in one piece. Dr. Sessions is all set to begin your—" she paused for a moment—"non-invasive testing tomorrow morning."

I stood up and started to leave, but something stopped me and I turned back to face Old Man Winter, who was still looking at me with that damned eerie stare. "You knew Wolfe would cut through your agents, didn't you?"

"That's a ridiculous assertion," Ariadne said from behind him. If he was insulted, he didn't show any more umbrage to it than anything else I'd said. "If we'd known this was going to happen we wouldn't have sent anyone, especially not you."

"Not what I asked," I replied. "And you're not who I asked. You offered to just send your agents because you didn't want to endanger me. So my question stands – you knew he would cut through them, yes? Not you, Ariadne." I pointed at her. "He overruled you."

Old Man Winter gazed back at me. "If Wolfe was there, it was certain that he would cut through any agents we sent."

I felt my mouth dry out at the words he spoke, and my voice quivered, just a little, as I whispered my next question. "Then why did you let us go?"

"Enough." Ariadne's words cut off his quiet reply, and she surged forward from her place behind him, putting a hand on my elbow and trying to escort me out the door. I restrained my impulse to flatten her. "You wanted to go, we helped you in exchange for your consent to test you—"

"No." I shook her hand off with almost no effort. "I need to know." I looked back at Old Man Winter, and he did not shy from my gaze. He held his hand up to stay Ariadne.

"Because you demanded it," he said with slow, measured words. "And you are more important to us than a hundred agents."

The blue eyes forced a chill in me as he answered, and they followed me unceasing as Ariadne led me from the room. This time I did not resist her.

Twelve

I parted from Ariadne after a muttered curse under my breath, leaving her with a shocked look (again). She lanced back with a scathing reminder about the testing, set for early tomorrow, at which point I left. If I could blame my antisocial behavior on Asperger's like some ridiculous TV character I would, but the truth is that I was trying my hardest not to think about the lives I had cost in my attempt to face off with Wolfe. And I was still struggling with who I could trust.

Old Man Winter had said I was more valuable to them than a hundred agents, but the question I had to ask was 'why?' I walked back to the dormitories using the above ground route, and when I walked out the doors of the headquarters building the icy sting of the wind lanced my cheeks.

I smelled that familiar scent hanging in the air again, that of a real wood fire, just like Mom used to build sometimes in our fireplace at home. We would actually make s'mores on it, like people in movies do when they're camping, and one time she got mad at me for breaking the rules and stuck my hand in the fire. True story. It had healed by the next day, but it hurt like hell, the flesh nearly peeling off the bone. That time was for the audacity to ask about how people lived in the outside world, breaking rule #5. Oops.

My eyes looked over the grounds and I found myself wondering what this place looked like in the middle of summer. Then my thoughts went back to the faces of those agents, in the garage when I met them, and I wondered what they did on a normal day, when they weren't escorting me to my house. Some of them had families, wives, kids. I didn't know a single one of their names.

It was only about four in the afternoon, but it was already getting dark. The haze of clouds hanging overhead was only making it worse. Still no sign of the sun, just like if I'd never left home. The wind was bitter, bad enough that even I didn't want to stay out for very long. After being cooped up inside for a decade, you'd think I'd want to spend as much time outside as possible – and I did, but there were limits, and apparently they were at three degrees Fahrenheit.

I entered the dormitory building to find people going about their business in the hallways, passing me with the occasional nod. I wondered if these people – metas, I thought – knew the agents that got killed. I wondered if they worked here or if they were just here for study, like me. I wondered what their lives were like, their stories, and if any of them missed their parents.

I opened the door to my room and didn't even bother to do a thorough check before I lay down. I grabbed a bottle of water from the fridge, twisted the cap and drank it without replacing it from the tap. Who cares? What were they going to do, poison me? Bring it on. I was at their mercy – I didn't trust them, but it wasn't like I had anywhere else to go.

Except I thought about Reed again, and about how I dreamed of him. I wondered if I could do it again. I put the water aside and lay down, thinking of him. I remembered his brown eyes, his hair framing his tan face, and I drifted off.

It felt like I lingered in the dark for hours before he showed up, fading into view a little at a time. He looked around and saw me, a look of unsurprise on his face.

"Hi." I waved, feeling more than a little stupid.

He lowered his head and shook it in something akin to deep disappointment. "You stirred up a hell of a hornet's nest."

I blinked at him, and wondered for a second why I would be blinking when my eyes were closed and I was asleep. "What do you mean?"

"I mean your showdown with Wolfe."

I looked away. "Yeah, I know. I got people killed."

"It's not that!" Reed said, incredulous. "Directorate agents die all the time. Whatever you did when you fought Wolfe, he's lost it. He's over the edge now."

"He wasn't before?"

Reed exploded. "This is no joking matter! He was going to capture you before, when he was following his employer's orders. Now he's lost it and they're panicking because he's gone rogue. He wants to kill you."

"How do you know that?" Little tingles of suspicion started inside me; my stomach churned, hinting at a feeling of betrayal.

"The people I work with have spies inside the group he was working for. You *really* pissed him off. What did you do?"

I shrugged, numb at the revelation. "Made him bleed."

Disappointed, Reed's hand found its way to his face. "Why did you go back to where you knew he could be?"

I clenched my jaw and felt pain, and thought about whether I must have been doing it in my sleep. "Because I didn't want to just sit here and stew in my fear of him. If you sit around and think about how much you're afraid of something, it just makes it worse. I didn't think he was that bad…I thought I could beat him." I lowered my head. "I was wrong."

"You *wanted* to face off with Wolfe?" He shook his head. "That's madness. You need to stay where you are, let the Directorate protect you."

"The Directorate can't protect me. He went through their agents like they were made of whipped cream."

"It doesn't matter, Sienna. I don't think he can touch you so long as you stay there."

"I don't want to stay here any more," I said. "I'm ready to leave and join you."

He shook his head again. "Sorry, but you can't do that. I can't protect you right now, not from Wolfe. Soon, but not right now."

"I just…" I crinkled my eyes, closing them as tight as I could. "I just want to get out of here. Out of town. Away from everything and everyone." I took a breath. "I read a book about towns in western South Dakota, and it had pictures; they were gorgeous, green and mountainous. I want to see mountains, Reed, and beaches, and anything but this gawdawful snow. It's so dim and dark all the time and I hate it…"

"This is not a problem you can run away from," he said with a look of sadness. "Wolfe is relentless."

"He doesn't know where I am now, and he can't know where I am from here on if I'm careful. My mom dodged these people for years. He's not a psychic and he's not infallible."

"You don't know Wolfe. He's lived for thousands of years and he uses time to his advantage. You're right: you'd likely make it out of the Minneapolis area, maybe even out of the state and the country, but he'd track you down eventually."

He wore a look of pity and I felt something sharp inside that woke up my defenses. I didn't know Reed any better than the Directorate people. I composed myself, pasting a smile that was as fake as any I'd ever worn. "Fine. All right."

"I can tell you're hurting…"

"You don't know anything about me," I snapped. Not sure where that came from, but I had a suspicion.

"Not much, but I can tell you're blaming yourself for what happened to those Directorate agents."

"I have to go," I replied, as brusque as I could make it. "I have to wake up. They're going to test me in the morning."

"Just make sure you—" His words faded as I struggled and forced my way out of the dream. I didn't wonder until later what he was going to say.

Thirteen

I woke up just after one in the morning. Except for a few minor aches, my injuries from the battle with Wolfe had healed themselves without much sign of anything odd. I realized I had gone to bed without dinner and that I hadn't eaten much lunch the day before either. I left my dormitory room (always fully dressed, remember?) and wandered the halls. I didn't hold much hope that the cafeteria would be open at this hour, but I doubted I would have a problem stealing some food.

Besides, was it really stealing? They would have given it to me if they'd been open. I came through the entrance to the cafeteria and found a few lights on, scattered throughout the place. Spotlights outside the massive windows showed snow was lightly falling outside. The smell of cleaning solutions hung in the air and when coupled with the dimness it gave the place the vague sense of what I'd imagine a hospital to feel like.

A lone figure was sitting in the corner where the two glass walls met, staring out into the dark. I crept up quietly until I got close enough to realize it was Zack, then started to tiptoe away. I didn't want to talk to anyone, least of all him.

"I can see your reflection," he called out. He turned, revealing a series of bandages over his nose with a piece of metal over it to hold it in place for healing. "I figured you'd be hungry sooner or later."

"Yeah," I replied. "Hungry and tired, so I think I'll just get something and go…"

"Why don't you sit down?" His eyes didn't let me retreat. They were watching me and I felt almost as helpless as when

Wolfe's black eyes were on me. I felt myself lower into the seat opposite him and he stared back at me as I did. I had the nasty feeling I knew what was coming next, but like a scene in a horror movie you don't want to watch but can't look away from, I was stuck in place.

"I want to talk about the basement." He was still watching me. I didn't like it. I hated it. I despise feeling trapped, and trapped I was. I hoped this would be quick – I hoped it was already over, actually, that maybe he didn't see as much as I thought he had, that he'd not bothered to report it to Ariadne or Old Man Winter, and definitely not Kurt.

"About the fight with Wolfe?" I tried to keep the hope out of my voice.

"You know that's not what I mean. Before him. What I saw…" His voice trailed off.

I remained silent. In a failed effort to be casual, I focused really, really hard on my left middle fingernail and started counting backward from one hundred.

"Sienna?" He repeated my name twice more in a bid to get my attention.

"I don't want to talk about this." My voice was quiet, but firm. Maybe a hint of a crack.

"You need to talk to somebody about it."

"No, I don't." I could feel myself get defensive, pissed. "I'm pretty much a full grown woman at this point, and I can make my own decisions about what I want to talk about and don't, and this falls into the territory of 'don't'."

"You were locked in a house for over ten years and you never escaped? With your mother gone to work all day, every day?" He shook his head. "I've been asking myself since we met how a mother could keep a kid in check that long, even if they were the most passive, easygoing person on the face of the planet—"

"I gather you're saying I'm not—"

"—let alone a stubborn, willful child that probably resisted from day one, just bucking for freedom any which way she could—"

I pursed my lips. "You make me sound like a wild horse."

"Let's go with that analogy," he said, nodding, which broke our eye contact. "How does someone domesticate a horse?"

"They break it," I said with a hint of defiance. "Do I look broken to you?"

"Looks don't mean a thing. She did break you, didn't she?"

I blew air out my lips and stared out the window at the snowfall. "I broke rules all the time," I said in a tone of forceful denial. "She wasn't home during the day, and I could do anything I wanted—"

"Except leave the house."

The wind outside kicked up and the snow started falling sideways. I hadn't seen that before. "No, I didn't leave the house, but I looked outside plenty of times."

He leaned across the table, making a bid to recapture my attention from the snow drifts that I allowed to distract me. "When she caught you breaking the rules, how did she punish you?"

I was stronger than him – I could have knocked him out and broken through a window and been gone. Gone from the Directorate and gone from this state and gone from my sorry little example of a stunted life. Tomorrow I could be living somewhere else and no one would catch me.

It was funny, because the cafeteria was hundreds of feet long and hundreds of feet wide, and the nearest table was ten steps away, and yet I felt like I was trapped in an enclosed space; it was just like…

"Yeah." My acknowledgment came out in a voice of surrender. "That was how."

In the corner of our basement stands a box. Made of

hardened steel plates an inch thick, welded together, it's a little over six feet tall, about two feet wide and two feet deep, when it stands long-end up. It opens like a coffin, along the longest plane. There's a sliding door on that side, about two inches tall and four inches wide, just enough to see out of – or into – the box. There are hinges on one side and a heavy locking peg on the other.

I knew when Zack saw it that he would figure it out. But it was worse when he opened it.

"She didn't let you out to...do your business?"

I shook my head. But he already knew the answer to that, because the smell inside it was horrific; it made the whole basement stink of rot when it was open.

"How long did she leave you in there?" His eyes still appeared unreactive.

I laughed, a dark, humorless bark that rumbled through me, keeping my emotions in check behind a facade of false bravado. "Which time? There were so many. As you mentioned, I am somewhat stubborn and defiant. I was in there at least once a week. Usually for smarting off; Mom didn't like that much."

"How long?"

I shrugged. "An hour or two, most of the time – with the door closed on the front, so it was completely dark. And that, honestly, wasn't so bad. It was the times when I was in there for days, those were the ones when it was bad—" The times when my stomach screamed at me because it was sick of nothing but the water that was piped in from a reservoir by a small tube. The times when I started to get lightheaded and had to sit down, where I just felt weak and near dead by the time she let me out.

If she let me out.

He grimaced, the first sign of emotion I'd seen from him since the conversation began. "What about the longest time?"

I paused, and an insane sounding laugh bubbled out of my mouth. I felt a stupid, pasted-on grin stretching my face. "A week,

I think."

His voice had grown quiet, but it was undergirded by a curiosity. "When was that?"

Silence owned me, but just for a beat. "Let's see. After I ate something and showered, I lay down to sleep – you know, horizontally, because trying to sleep curled up in a ball inside it sucks, just FYI – and I woke up and you and Kurt were in my house. So…a few days ago."

This time the silence was stunned. "She left you…after locking you in?"

I nodded, hoping he wouldn't ask the dark, piteous question I'd been asking myself lately. "And I haven't seen her since."

Fourteen

That ended Zack's questions, thank God. He said some more things after that, but I missed pretty much all of it. My head was buzzing and I couldn't focus. I forgot that I was hungry and as soon as I could get away from him I did, leaving him in the cafeteria. He extracted a promise from me that we would talk more soon, and I didn't argue because I didn't have the energy.

Ever been in a fight that gets really emotional, and you may have been feeling absolutely wonderful five minutes earlier but suddenly you're just exhausted? That was me; all my energy was shot and I dragged myself back to my dormitory. I crashed on my bed, but I didn't fall asleep. Instead I thought about Mom again; of the last time I saw her, when she shut the door on me, even as I was screaming, hammering my palms against the steel and begging her not to – and then she peered at me through the little sliding door, her eyes looking into mine, and she said something different than the hundreds of other times she'd put me in.

"Whatever you may think, I do this all for your own good." I wasn't in a position to pay attention at the time (I was as distressed when I went into the box as a cat being dunked in water – I've seen it on TV) but her look was different than usual. Less spiteful. Less vengeful. Less pissed. I might have seen a trace of sadness in her eyes, though I didn't recognize it at the time.

Then she shut the little door and left me in the darkness.

I thought about her again, concentrating hard, trying to focus on her as I drifted off to sleep. I awoke the next morning, an alarm going off beside the bed. I hadn't set it, but it was blaring. I looked at the clock and realized it was timed so I didn't miss my appointment with Dr. Sessions. Someone from the Directorate must have done it, fearing (probably rightly) that I didn't much care if I made them wait. Probably Ariadne. That bitch.

I thought about blowing it off, but the truth is I was curious. After all, they kept telling me I was meta-human, and I believed it, but I wondered what other abilities I might have. I was hoping for flight, because that would be cool.

When I got to Dr. Sessions's office, he was sitting behind his desk, looking at something. When he heard me enter he turned and pushed his glasses back up his nose and looked through them at me. "There you are." He began nodding and picked up a tablet computer that sat next to the laptop on the desk. "Have a seat; I need to have you fill out this questionnaire before we begin…" He handed me a clipboard and pen, then turned to walk away. I gave him a quick smile of thanks, which caused him to back away. I sighed internally. Even when I wasn't trying to, I could drive people away from me.

The questionnaire took an annoyingly long time and asked some invasive personal questions ("How many sexual encounters have you had in the last seven days? Two weeks? Month? Six months? Year? Five years?") Not like it was a difficult one, since until a few days ago I'd had zero human contact outside of Mom.

There were other ones that delved into health history, how I was feeling, when was the date of my last physical ("Never!" I printed in big, bold letters), when I first noticed a difference in my abilities – and on it went for a hundred and fifty questions, covering both the important ("Do you have any known allergies?") to the mundane ("When was your last bowel movement?"). I thought about scrawling "None of your damned business" but ultimately I just answered the questions – almost all – truthfully.

The last question – "Describe in detail any unusual abilities or skills" – gave me pause. Part of me wanted to know more, to find out what kind of meta I was. Okay, all of me wanted to know.

But that was tempered by the fact that I had only been here for three days and still had zero idea of who (if anyone) I could trust. If I told them I suspected I could use my dreams to communicate with others, would that be considered some kind of power or a sign that I was slipping in the sanity department? I believed I could talk to Reed through my dreams, but it was too weird to consider normal and as yet too unconfirmed for me to know with certainty I could do it. After all, it could have been his power, not mine.

I answered the question, "Superior Strength, Speed, Agility and Intelligence" (no, I didn't put a smiley next to the intelligence part) and left any other suspicions off. As I had filled out the form, the doctor had milled around the lab, adjusting various pieces of equipment, humming as he skittered about.

He noticed me after a minute or so, and favored me with a smile as he approached. "We're going to do some physical tests next, then I'll give you this – a standard, multiple choice I.Q. test – and we'll see how you do."

For the next three hours, he put me through my paces. I thought maybe I had pissed him off in some way, because he was not kind in his efforts to "test" me. I ran on a treadmill at the highest setting for a long time, well past the point where I was bored and into the realm of thinking of casting myself into the place where the tread meets the plastic at the back, hoping to end my life with the added benefit that perhaps the running would stop as well. It couldn't have been an ordinary treadmill because I swear I had to be running at fifty miles an hour.

He made me breathe into a machine (to test my lung capacity), had me lift weights (I cursed him because there was no measure of how much they weighed and he refused to tell me) and hit a punching bag. Then he handed me rubber balls and had me throw them at a target on a wall at full strength, which I did (until I turned all three of them into pancakes).

"It would have been easier if you would have taken your gloves off," he said, looking over his glasses at me.

"Sorry, Doc. Rule number four."

A look of confusion swept over his face. He led me over to a table in the corner. "One last thing." He bade me to sit.

"The intelligence test?"

"Two more things. First—" He reached onto the table and picked up a needle along with a strip of rubber. "I need blood."

My eyes narrowed. "I would suggest trying your local blood bank, because you'll get none from me."

He didn't smile. "In order to analyze—"

"Test what you have, Doc," I said in a voice that I hoped didn't allow for argument, "if none of that pans out, we'll talk about a blood draw in the future."

He stood there for a moment, looking like he was a broken robot, his head shaking in a twitchy fashion while he tried to come up with a response. He must have failed, because he never said anything, just tossed the I.Q. test on the table and shuffled away.

I attacked the test with a certain frustration. It was easy, and I used the pen provided to violently circle my answers on the multiple choice form. As I did, thoughts of the agents I had gotten killed kept running through my head. Zack had worked with all of them. He didn't seem that bent out of shape by the fact they were dead.

Kurt did. That was an honest reaction. Hannegan had already disliked me; now he hated me. I circled answer D, responding to a question about square roots, bringing the pen around to give it an extra loop, and nearly tore through the paper. Whoops. Gotta be careful with super strength, I guess.

But Zack? He was more concerned about things that happened to me (an almost total stranger) instead of worrying about his co-workers being dead because of me. I came to the conclusion that he had to be planted. Like Ariadne, he was restraining his emotions, putting them in the backseat to focus on the job at hand. Had to be.

Which meant Ariadne and Old Man Winter probably told him to get close to me, because he was the nearest to my age of all their people. And hot. H-O-T. Ariadne may be dumb, but I doubted she was blind enough to miss that little fact. And Old Man Winter himself said I was more important than a hundred of their agents.

That was a harrowing boost to the ego, let me tell you. There wasn't much on the I.Q. test about history, which was a shame because it was one of my best subjects. It wasn't the first time in history someone's life had been prioritized over another's. Not even close. But when I heard him say it, it started to worry me about the Directorate.

It got me wondering if they were some sort of racial superiority group, focused on putting meta-humans into a power position. Or maybe Old Man Winter was just that screwed up in his priorities, that he could cast a hundred human lives aside without losing any sleep over it.

Or maybe he was losing sleep over it. It wasn't like I knew him well enough to tell.

I finished the last question and looked around for the doc, but he was gone. He must have walked out while I was focused on the test. I left it on the table and walked out of the lab, heading out into the cold air thinking I might finally get that meal I had been craving since last night. A blast of windblown snow hit me in the face as I left the lab and hiked across the campus. I marveled at how smooth it looked.

I found the cafeteria crammed for breakfast. In fact, based on the size of the room there had to be at least a couple hundred people in there. I had only visited in off-peak times so to see it full was quite the surprise. There were men in suits scattered through the room, as well as other men and women dressed in work attire of various sorts, and a smattering of people I assumed were metas dressed in casual clothes, jeans, t-shirts, most of them younger than the folks dressed professionally.

As I walked to where the line formed to get food, my stomach rumbled. It coincided with a hush falling over the cafeteria – a slow, steady lowering of the volume level. I got a tray and began filling it. I was hungry, and not for broccoli. As I worked my way to the end of the line I started to overhear murmurings from both the workers behind the counter and people talking in the rest of the cafeteria.

"...that's her..."

"...got all those agents killed..."

"...heard some crazed meta named Wolfe is hunting her..."

"...she did it on purpose..."

"...eight of them dead, almost got Kurt and Zack too..."

"...crazy bitch."

The last one caught my attention, but I restrained myself before I whipped around to confront whoever had said it. I realized my hearing had not gotten sensitive, that most of the people were speaking loud enough for me to hear them. Which meant they were looking for a reaction. My eyes scanned the crowd as I left the line with my tray. The professionally dressed people looked away. About ninety percent of the folks in casual dress did likewise if they saw me look at them; a quick, furtive glance here and there if they got "caught."

But a few of the men in suits – the agents – were speckled throughout the crowd, and their looks were hard, hiding behind furrowed brows and cold eyes. And a small contingent of the casually dressed – the metas – were glaring and not bothering to hide it. They were all concentrated around one table.

I stared back at them, defiant. Yeah, I screwed up. But good luck getting me to admit it in public. I didn't bat an eye as their ringleader, a young guy probably only a few years older than me, gave me the stare-down right back. He had short dark hair and a nose that rounded a little at the end. The look of spite in his eyes overpowered his other features, turning what might otherwise have been a nice smile into something that looked more like a downward facing crescent moon.

I saw a small table empty in the far corner where the two windowed walls met each other – maybe the last unoccupied table in the place. Not a friendly face in sight, just a lot of people shunning me and a few more that were clearly pissed. Perfect. I pondered just carrying my tray out the door and back to my room where I could eat in comfortable solitude, but something in me resisted it.

I'd been alone for years. Locked away, trapped, whatever. It didn't bother me if I had to eat by myself. In a lot of ways, especially right now, doing that would have been the easiest choice. But still, my brain resisted the notion, urging me to not let these people get to me, to not run away and hide.

So when I picked my path to the empty table I made sure it went right past the group of metas that were scowling me down.

I waited to see if they would speak as I approached. I even pondered being a real ass and inviting myself to sit down in one of the empty seats at their table, but decided against it. I may not have been looking to make friends, but I didn't want to actively cultivate enemies if I didn't have to.

I just wanted to…confront them. Just a bit.

I almost didn't get my wish. They kept silent and a few even broke off their glares as I approached. I returned each hostile look in kind, until finally I rested my eyes once more on the young man: the ringleader, judging by the vibe I was getting off him. He didn't look away. He was waiting to see if I'd flinch.

I didn't. But neither did he. He stood up as I passed. Damn. Thought I was gonna make it by.

"Hey," he called out. "Friends of mine got killed on your

stupid errand."

"I'm sorry about your friends," I said with an astounding level of calm for the tension I was feeling inside. I think I meant it.

"'Sorry' doesn't bring them back." His glare was piercing.

"Neither does anything else I can do." The acerbic edge to my statement was probably what pissed him off. "Unless I have some amazing powers of resurrection I have yet to discover."

His look got angrier, thanks to narrowed eyes and a snarl on his lips. "They stuck their necks out for you."

"Far be it from me to suggest otherwise. But they also died doing the jobs that they took on, that Old Man Winter sent them to do. They knew there was a risk Wolfe could be there." I had stopped my forward motion and waited for Mr. Angry to reply. Might as well get this out of the way, and if I was lucky I could get the entire cafeteria off my back in one move.

"So you're one of the self-superior metas that gives the rest of us a bad name." His arms were folded across his body. "Don't really care if a bunch of humans die, so long as you get what you want."

I had a feeling that one was going to sting later but for now I pushed it aside and focused on my reply. "That's not what I said."

His chin jutted out. "But it's what you meant."

"Oh, is your power to read minds? No? Then don't tell me what I meant." I looked back at him with a gut full of defiance. I'd likely be blaming myself again later for the deaths, but I wasn't going to let him burn me with it; not now. "If I could do it all over again, I wouldn't have gone back. But I can't and I have to live with what happened. And you can take your rage and fire it up your ass."

He didn't say anything, but his jaw hardened and his nostrils flared. I realized that the pretense of standing there if I wasn't looking for a fight was pretty flimsy, so I made my way to the table. I sat down and looked out the window, trying to ignore all the stares from behind me.

A figure came up from behind a few minutes later and slid the chair out without asking. I was ready to gripe when I looked up. "Oh, it's you."

Zack sat down. "What are you doing here?" He cast an almost furtive look around. People were still staring. "It's not the most comfortable environment to be eating your lunch in, is it?"

I took another forkful of beef and chewed it while I pondered my response. "You mean because everyone in the room hates me?"

"That's not true," he said. "I don't hate you."

"Kudos to you for being the only one." I feigned applause for a couple beats before reaching down with my fork and spearing a bite of stray roast with unnecessary force. "So this is what being the school outcast would have felt like. I didn't really miss much being locked away all these years." My voice quavered and came out much lower. "Not that it matters."

"It doesn't matter if anybody likes you?" His voice carried a hint of skepticism.

"Nope. I've lived my entire life without the approval of any of these people. I suspect I can live the rest of it the same." I stabbed another piece of beef. "Especially considering how short it's likely to be."

"We can protect you from Wolfe if you stay," he said, his tone soothing.

"Oh boy," I said with mock enthusiasm. "I can spend the rest of my life wandering the halls of this place, feeling useless and listless and trapped, just like when I was at home – except here I'm surrounded by people who hate me." As if to punctuate my statement, I pushed my tray away. I was done.

"At least nobody here will lock you in a metal box for days at a time," he replied, a touch defensive.

"My entire life is boxes." I twirled the fork before setting it down on my discarded plate. "First I was trapped in my house or in the box; now I'm trapped on your campus. Most people are trapped in their towns, or their jobs, or their way of life. We go through life in our little boxes until we find ourselves in the last one, buried in the ground."

My tone was rueful, and I didn't care how general I was being. I was in a foul, depressive mood. I suspected that this guy, the only one in my life to ever show an interest in me (other than Reed, I guess), was doing it to spy on me for his boss, and I found myself longing for the simplicity of my house, where at least I knew where I stood. Act out, Mom gets pissed and I get stuck in the box. Simple.

He pushed back from the table. "That's a bit—"

"'A bit' what? Accurate? Morbid?" I laughed. "It's a bit irrelevant. I'll stay here, milking the security of your Directorate for all it's worth, because I've got nowhere else to go and there's no way I can beat Wolfe. So I'll wait, and bide my time, and hope that when your much vaunted M-Squad comes back they can find a way to kill him so I can at least have the luxury of deciding where I want to go and what I want to do with the rest of my life."

"It doesn't have to be this way." His voice was soft, almost lost in the din of the cafeteria conversations. "You could work with us here, build a life at the Directorate."

"And what? Join M-Squad? Be a test subject? Hang out like all these other metas, waiting for – what? I don't even know what they do here!" My hand gesticulated toward the table of metas that had accosted me earlier. "Part of me just wants to go home. And the rest of me…" My voice cracked.

"What?" He leaned forward but kept his hands far from mine. I could see the intensity in his eyes, the concern, and it just pissed me off all the more because I was so sure it was fake and I wanted it to be real, more than anything. "What do you want?"

I froze, and I knew in that moment I was on the brink of

tears. *Suck it up*, I told myself. I took a moment to compose my emotions, shoving them into the back of my mind. I'm tough. I made the decision not to let even an ounce of feeling into my voice. "I don't know." It came out more brittle than I would have hoped, but it still sounded strong. "And it doesn't matter right now, because my only priority is survival." He nodded almost sadly as I stood up. "Everything else comes later."

I left the cafeteria, head in a spin. I waited around my room for a while, not really sure what to do. There was a flatscreen TV hanging from the wall, but I didn't see a point in watching anything. I didn't really miss it that much after not watching for a few days.

I settled on going to the gym, which I did in spite of the fact that Dr. Sessions had paired me with the treadmill from hell earlier. I stuck with a recumbent bike for my self-directed cardio, and whaled on a heavybag that a trainer assured me was made especially for metas (she told me this with a very friendly attitude until someone came up and whispered to her, at which point her disposition matched the weather outside). So I hit the heavybag even harder, punishing it for every bad decision I'd made lately, imagining the face of that guy in the cafeteria as I belted it another one, then wished I could pound Wolfe like I was pounding it. Unfortunately, Wolfe hit back.

After I finished I went back to my room and showered. I checked the time and found that it was mid-afternoon. I hung around a little longer. Someone had left me an e-reader. After reading for an hour or so I realized it was basically the same as a book but more convenient, and the novelty wore off. I've read lots of books.

At four thirty I decided I could get dinner and that it'd be early enough to dodge most of the crowd at the cafeteria. Besides, the sun would be down by 5:30, so I might as well be ready to sleep when it got dark. I decided I'd try and dream of Mom or

Reed again. Probably Mom, since I wanted to prove I could contact others in their dreams and I'd talked to Reed twice already.

The cafeteria was near empty, and I snaked as much food as I could, keeping a careful watch on what went on my plate. It's not that I thought the workers would do something evil; it's just I've seen enough on TV detailing what wait staff do to the food of people they don't like to make me paranoid. It adds another dimension to being hated.

The dinner was chicken, and it was good. I managed to creep out of the dining hall just as it started to get busy. A few poisonous looks and some stage-whispered comments that lacked originality were my reward for lingering too long. A hall clock told me it was 5:45. The sun, which I still hadn't seen, was either down or the cloud cover it was hiding behind was thick, because it was dark outside.

I paused by a window in the corridor outside my room and stared across the grounds. What would Mom think of all this? I wondered. Where was she? Why did she leave? I swallowed hard. What caused her to flee? Was she in trouble?

Was it me?

The smells of dinner filled my nose as the volume of the crowd in the cafeteria was on a steady rise, so loud now I could hear them from where I was on the other side of the building. Most of the professionals had gone home for the day, but the casually dressed metas passed me in the hall, on their way to evening meal. Their conversations were excited, those of people among friends, and they dropped off when they saw me.

I realized I had been staring out the window at a lamp for the last five minutes. Going to the gym to work out again didn't appeal to me, and I had a feeling Dr. Sessions wouldn't be getting back with my results this evening. I thought of Mom again and knew that what I wanted was to go to sleep and try to dream of her.

I walked down the hall to my door and opened the handle. It wasn't locked, because I didn't have a key for it. Since everyone hated me, I supposed I should get a key, so that no one could sneak into my room while I was away.

I closed the door and flipped the light switch and realized that I was, by far, too late, because not only had someone snuck in while I was at dinner, but they had stayed to wait for me.

"Hello, little doll," came the whispered, throaty voice of Wolfe, towering above me. His hand came down and grabbed me around the neck while I was still too stunned to react. "Wolfe has been waiting for you." He pulled me close to him and I felt his hot, stinking breath on my face, then felt the warm wetness of his tongue licking my cheek. "It's time to play."

Fifteen

However I might have responded, speech was not possible with his hand squeezing my larynx. His black eyes were bulging out and his smile was a grin that revealed his spiked teeth. I felt them brush against the side of my head as he pulled me close and took a long breath through his nose, inhaling on my hair.

"Wolfe has missed you twice, little doll, but now we can be together and play the way we're supposed to. Then, whatever's left of you when Wolfe is done…" I felt his breath drift down to my neck as he embraced me and his teeth slightly bit into my shoulder – enough to puncture the cloth of my turtleneck and the skin but not enough to cause a deep wound – and a little sucking sound followed for about a second. "…*they* can have. That will make them happy. And you…will make Wolfe happy first." A half-insane titter of glee came from him and I heard the smacking of his lips.

I made a guttural sound of choking and he loosened his grip as he moved me in front of him, enough so I could take a breath but not much more. I could already feel the pins and needles in my feet and I tried not to jerk too much for fear of breaking my own neck. I must not have been the first person he'd placed in a chokehold because he'd learned to grip low enough on the neck that he didn't cut off all circulation.

"Pl…pl…" I couldn't get a word out.

He turned me around in his hand so that he was behind me. I could feel his body pressed against me, as though it were an iron wall at my back. My feet touched the floor again but his grip assured me that if I tried anything out of line, I wouldn't survive until the agents came to my rescue. Not that they would at this point. Not after what I did. I was alone here.

"Pl...please..." I rasped through the barest opening he gave me to speak.

I could hear a moan of pleasure. "Yessss, little doll. Begging is good play. Pleading is fun." His other hand crept around my waist and I felt a shudder of revulsion when it came to rest on my belly and one of his claws raked through my clothing, giving me another superficial laceration.

I felt a twinge of pain, sharp despite the shallowness of the cut, and I felt the trickle of blood start to run down my abdomen under my sweater. His finger ran to his mouth and I heard the sucking sound again followed by another little moan of pleasure that made me ill. "I can taste everything about you in your blood. Your fears. Your doubts...every exquisite little part of you...this will be satisfying for both of us..." His hand slid around my belly again and I grunted, my fear for my life momentarily outweighed by a rising sense of disgust.

"H-how..." The words stumbled out as my mind sought out any delay I could find. "How did you find me?"

His grip tightened and once more I found myself in a battle to breathe. "It's not your place to speak or ask questions. You are to be silent except for the occasional moan or scream." His fingers dug into the cut he had made in my stomach and it suddenly wasn't superficial anymore. I would have screamed, but he had a choking grip on my neck, as though he anticipated it.

"I'll tell you," I heard him say through the searing agony in my guts. "You shouldn't have left all those agents lying around when you ran from Wolfe last time...two of them were alive, you know...and very helpful, after Wolfe spent some time playing with them...very helpful...and tasty. They were no little dolls, but they made a fine distraction until I could get my hands around you...and in you..." He stabbed his finger back into me and I wanted to scream but was out of air. Lights blurred my vision and the edges of everything in the world smoothed out. A flash of light blinded me.

I felt a spasming shock of pain, lighter somehow than what was going on in my guts but still painful, and I felt his grip loosen. Another flash, another shock and his hand slipped from my neck. My hands found their way to my belly to staunch the bleeding. It felt like he had torn loose my intestines and I crumpled into a pile on the floor just trying to catch my breath. My eyes made their way up to an astounding sight.

The windows had exploded inward and men in black tactical vests swarmed the room, guns firing all around me. The one in front that was a little too small for his tactical equipment was blasting away with the same type of weapon I had seen Kurt use at my house. With a shock I realized it was Hannegan, his gear tight on his massive frame. Wolfe seemed to be resisting the weapon even more fiercely this time, shrugging off the shots. Shotguns were going off in cascading blasts of thunder in front of me, the muzzle flashes lighting the room.

A scream from Wolfe seemed to stop time and I saw a blur of motion from his hands as he lunged forward. Kurt went flying, hitting the wall and bouncing off, landing in a heap on three of his fellows. He was lucky; Wolfe had punched him rather than using his claws.

The next hit from Wolfe was a slash and it caught two guys with shotguns that had closed on him. One of them lost his head, literally, while the other started gushing blood from the chest. Wolfe lashed out with a kick in the other direction and I heard it make contact with a Directorate agent standing above me, just out of my field of vision. There was a sickening crunch of flesh and bone drawing and breaking, then a desperate sucking sound that tapered off after three breaths; it was audible to me only because he landed less than a foot to my right. I dared not look at the dying agent for fear of who it might be.

My hand clutched at my wounded stomach and I tried to get up on all fours but failed, lying prone on the ground. I saw another body hit the floor in front of me and realized that there was only one pair of feet still standing and it was the booted set belonging to Wolfe. I raised my head to look up at him as he stopped in front of me. He looked down with a twisted anticipation that made me feel nausea that had little to do with the fact that I was nearly gutted.

"Now..." he breathed, lifting me into the air, twisting my torso and wrenching a scream from my lips. "Before we were so rudely interrupted..." His finger hovered in front of my eyes and he twisted me around and laid me facedown on the bed. The pressure of his hands around my neck hurt as his claws pricked through my sweater and drew blood. I felt him standing above me even though my face was buried in the bed. I screamed again but it was so muffled by the mattress that it didn't even sound that loud in my head.

He wrenched me around, twisting my midsection once more and then forcibly placing an arm over my upper body, anchoring me in place. "Much better," he said in a whisper. "Now I can hear you scream."

I'm ashamed to say that the next sound I made was more of a whimper. At least if I screamed defiance I could have vented some emotion in his direction. As it was, the panic was so rooted in me that I had no idea what I could do about it. He was invincible, I was wounded, everything hurt. I'd watched a whole army of trained agents go up against him and lose. What could I do? He rolled me to the right and then left, enjoying the squealing sounds I made from the pain in my stomach when he moved me. I was crying from the agony; it was horrific and I just wanted it to end.

The bedspread was slick with blood by this point, and he pushed me again. I caught a glimpse of a notebook and pen as he climbed up onto the bed and straddled me, looking down, one hand at his side and the other being used to completely manhandle me. I flopped about, offering little resistance. The pain was so bad I felt like I'd been cut in half. The best I could do was let him flip me again and maintain enough presence of mind to let my hand go to the pen on the nightstand, grasping hold of it.

"Grr...uckle..." I made a pathetic kind of gurgling noise that was about 90% from the pain that was starting to dull as I verged on passing out and about 10% from being unable to articulate the terror, agony and rage that flooded through me with the adrenaline.

"Tsk-tsk, little doll...I told you, your place is not to talk...it takes Wolfe out of the moment..."

I made another gurgling sound as I tried to speak. I wish I could say I had some witty remark in mind, but I was far beyond that point. I was just trying to get him to hold up for a moment, to get him to listen to me.

It worked. "What's that, little doll?" He leaned in close, tongue running along my cheek. "We're destined to be interrupted any time, so perhaps Wolfe should finish now? Or perhaps carrying you away will heighten the anticipation for later?" His free hand pawed my chest, bringing a fresh wave of nausea as he took liberties with me that no one had ever taken before.

"Not...like...this...!" I spat a mouthful of blood in his face, causing him to recoil as I brought the pen up and around, driving it into his ear. His hand was already moving to wipe off the spit when the pen made contact. I didn't have much strength left, but I used it all and aimed it perfectly. It sunk in and he tore off a scream that sounded like the world was ending in front of my face; then he hauled off and backhanded me so hard I flopped off the bed, landing on the floor facedown.

"BITCH!" His fury was white-hot and I could hear him above me. At this point I was immobile, unable to move anything but my hands, which had found their way to my stomach wound. "I'm going to finish you now, and I'm not even going to be nice, little doll. There won't be anything left when I'm done with you—"

His hands seized me on the shoulders and he rubbed my face into the carpet hard enough that my nose broke. I felt him clutching at me, scratching and cutting as he used his claws to hack at the waistband of my pants – then I heard another horrific cracking noise and it took me a minute to realize that the sound wasn't made by him hitting me but by someone else hitting him.

A blast of chill ran through the room from the window and I could have sworn that there was a winter storm even though a few minutes earlier it had only been cloudy. A gust blew in a circle and I realized my door was open. The breath of frost licked at me and the feeling of a deep chill ran up my spine, causing me to wonder if it was from the blood loss. The cold wind carried its own smell, unique, but a subtle reminder of the walks I had taken around the grounds in the last few days.

I used the last of my strength to roll to my back and realized I was surrounded by the prostrate bodies of the agents that had stormed the room. My eyes moved to Wolfe, on one knee, still impossibly tall, but faced down by a dark figure that stood between him and me. Wolfe was breathing in fits and crimson ran down the side of his face in a dark stream from his ear. "Jotun," he said in a low voice. "You're still alive after all these centuries."

"Only just," came the quiet voice of Old Man Winter. His height was not quite that of Wolfe when the beast was standing, but seemed like a giant from my perspective. "The millenia have been kinder to you than to me, I'm afraid."

"Let me have the girl," Wolfe said, dragging himself to his feet. "You can have the little doll back when I'm done, but I have to...have to...finish...I can even leave her alive when I'm done...at least a little..."

"I think not," Old Man Winter said without pause. "I have another squad of agents on the way, and you know that with my help..." He let his words trail off.

"I'm not done with her." Wolfe's voice was infused with a kind of mania that chilled me worse than the freezing air. He stomped his foot and I heard a snap that I suspected was the sound of his foot finding a Directorate agent's neck as it landed. "I won't stop until I have her, 'til we...play." The last words came out in a twisted, lyrical note that would have filled me with disgust if I weren't completely wrecked.

"You are done with her," Old Man Winter said as the chill intensified, both from his words and from a howling tempest of cold winds. "You will not seek her here again unless you wish to face me...and as old as I am now, you and I both know that although one may survive a confrontation between the two of us, the survivor would never be the same..."

I thought I saw a brief tremor from Wolfe, but it faded as his eyes flickered and the most horrifying creature I could ever imagine bounded out the window. I heard the crushing of snow for a few footfalls, saw Old Man Winter turn to face me with those ice blue eyes, and then it was as if my brain blissfully proclaimed me safe, because I lowered myself back down and passed out.

Sixteen

When I woke up, things were hazy and a small woman was hovering over me in a lab coat. She flashed me a quick smile as I blinked at her. "Don't try and sit up yet," she said, brushing a lock of black hair out of her eyes as she leaned over me. I obeyed her, mostly because I didn't feel as if I could move. I looked down to see my clothes replaced with a hospital gown.

The memory of Wolfe's attack cut through the haze and I felt nausea set in below the pain in my stomach. I started to gag as I recalled every sickening detail of what he tried to do to me and I began to retch. Searing pain raced through my abdomen.

"Whoa!" The woman grasped me under my shoulders, helping me turn. I threw up over the edge of the table, unable to control my reaction. A disgusting feeling of being violated seeped into me and I retched again. I wanted to shower, to scrub my skin until it bled. I grimaced from the pain in my stomach that was made worse by my heaving. "You need to settle down. That maniac nearly pulled out your intestines and that'll slow anyone down, even a fast-healing meta like yourself."

I coughed. "Who are you?"

She wrapped a stethoscope around her neck before answering. "Dr. Isabella Perugini. I'm the resident M.D. here in the medical unit."

I blanched as she turned and injected a needle in an IV that ran to my arm. "Where's Dr. Sessions?"

She snorted. "The lab rat is where he belongs – playing with test tubes and beakers."

The haze of pain began to lift. It was still there; I just didn't notice it as much. "So he doesn't treat patients?"

"No." She turned back to me, a clipboard in her hands. "I've treated you both times you've come through my doors. Want some medical advice?"

"Will it stop the pain?"

"Not immediately, but it could prevent it in the future." She turned serious. "Stop facing off with this Wolfe character, will you? I'm sick of having blood all over my floor."

"Send some of it to your pal Dr. Sessions; he's jonesing for it."

"First of all, it's not all yours," she said with a nod to a half dozen figures on beds down a line from me. The agents that tried to rescue me from Wolfe. "Second, if he wants it, Ron's welcome to come over here with a mop; I suspect the janitorial department is getting quite sick of cleaning up these sorts of messes."

"Did someone say my name?" I looked as far as I could toward the doorway and saw Dr. Sessions silhouetted in the frame.

"Yeah," I said in a ragged whisper. "I was just telling Dr. Perugini that she should save you some of my excess blood since it's everywhere."

"Yes," he said with excitement, "that would be marvelous."

"Ron," Dr. Perugini said in acknowledgment, with a tone that indicated some impatience. "Why are you darkening my door?"

"I came to give Ms. Nealon her test results." His face twitched and he pushed the glasses back up into position on his nose. "Quite interesting."

"Of course it escapes your notice she's near dead," Perugini muttered under her breath, sparking a quizzical look from Sessions. She opened her arms wide. "By all means, deliver your test results."

"So what am I?" I said without preamble.

"No idea," he replied as he crossed the floor and halted at my bedside. "You defy immediate classification." A smile of delight colored his pasty features. "Truly bizarre."

"He's a sweet talker, that one," I said to Dr. Perugini, who snorted again, this time in amusement. "Why is that bizarre?"

"I've analyzed hundreds of meta-humans," he went on, "and most fall into common types – a half-dozen or so groupings depending on the special powers they exhibit. Some tend more toward incredible physical attributes, some have energy projection capabilities or—"

"Perhaps speak to the girl in English," Dr. Perugini interrupted.

"No need for that," he corrected her. "I gave her an intelligence test as well; I could be having this discussion in Latin and she'd pick up the essential points. The simple fact is—"

"I defy classification," I interrupted, my words calm, coming out over the foul, acidic taste in my mouth from my recent bout of vomiting. "Even among the bizarre, I'm bizarre."

A phone rang across the medical unit and Dr. Perugini gave Dr. Sessions a thinly lidded glare before striding away to answer it. He kept his distance, as though he were uncomfortable stepping any closer. Instead he stared at me in a way that, had any other man done it right now, would likely have set me to vomiting again. I stared back at him. "What?"

"Your physical strength is high above a normal meta's, so you should be manifesting soon, if you haven't already. No unique abilities to report yet?" I felt zero compunction about lying, but was relieved that Dr. Perugini had stepped away; I suspected she would see through my untruth; Dr. Sessions didn't have a prayer.

"No. Nothing unusual."

He turned back to his clipboard. "Well, that's fine…it's normal that you wouldn't be experiencing anything yet. But as time goes by, additional abilities will materialize." He looked down at the blood pooled at his feet. "And I'll, uh…" He pulled a small test tube out of his coat pocket and stooped down, scraping it across the tile floor, forcing a small amount into the vial before putting a rubber stopper on it. Dr. Perugini rounded the corner just in time to see him and threw up her hands in silent exasperation.

He stood up, failing to notice her behind him. "I'll get this analyzed and maybe it'll give us some ideas of what you are." He turned and started when he saw Dr. Perugini, then shuffled around her as she glared at him.

"He has the bedside manner of a goat," she said with a hint of a European accent. "But not the common sense nor tact. That—" she pointed to the phone behind her—"was Ariadne. She and Old Man Winter are coming down to see you now that you're awake."

"Did they already know I was awake when they called?" I asked. I could believe Dr. Sessions would wander over and not know that I was unconscious; I'd be shocked if Ariadne and Old Man Winter weren't spying on me.

She stared back at me, her dark eyes cool and unflinching. "Yes." She turned away, grabbing a clipboard off a nearby shelf. "You're going to need to start eating again soon. I don't want to strain your digestive tract until I'm sure it's fully healed, so I'll be giving you another ultrasound in a couple hours to confirm you mend as fast as I suspect you do. After that, dinner will be served."

"I'm not hungry," I said. The brush with Wolfe made me wonder if I'd ever be able to eat again without heaving.

"That's okay," she replied without looking up from her clipboard. "I'm not feeding you yet."

The medical unit was a long room, probably as long as my house but narrower, with curtains separating individual beds and a private room at the far end with an oversized door for rolling gurneys in. Every surface was the same flat metal that I'd seen in the room I'd woken up in when I'd first arrived at the Directorate, broken up by glass windows that looked out into a hallway that matched the distinct look of the headquarters building.

The sharp odor of disinfectants wrinkled my nose as I took it in for the first time, almost giving me another reason to gag. I could hear the low beeps of monitoring equipment in the background and the faint hum of all the machinery. I counted the number of occupied beds I could see from where I lay. Less than a half dozen. "How do you handle so many at one time?" I asked.

"I don't," she said, a slight tremble in her voice. "I had to triage, and Old Man Winter demanded I treat you first."

"But I can survive more than any of them."

"I know," she said with a nod, not looking up from her clipboard. "And once I had established your wounds were not of the life-threatening variety, I moved on to the next critical patient."

"How many of them died?" The words were like ashes in my mouth. Bitter.

A moment of silence passed between us. "Five."

I did not respond to her statement, and she didn't speak either. The doors on the far side of the medical unit opened to admit Ariadne, who looked drawn, her severe suit wrinkled as though she had slept in it. Old Man Winter followed a pace behind her, his age less obvious today, I thought – or was that because I knew he wasn't what he appeared?

"Hello," Ariadne said. I didn't bother to glare. She took this as an invitation to move closer, and hovered over my bed. "How are you feeling?"

"Like I've been kicked, punched, gutted, slapped and stomped on," I said without much feeling. "So basically like you look all the time." I couldn't stop myself. Ouch.

Her jaw dropped only a little, and she recovered quickly. I think she was getting used to my barbs. Good. Old Man Winter stood a few feet behind her, watching me, but did not speak.

Ariadne looked chastened, but began again. "We've been keeping updated on your progress through Dr. Perugini. She's most impressed with your healing abilities, which rate very high on the meta-human scale."

"That's coming in handy more often than I would have hoped," I replied. "I take it Wolfe breaking into your dormitory building came as a surprise for you, too?"

Ariadne folded her arms and shook her head. "We shouldn't have taken Kurt's report that all our agents at your house were dead at face value; we should have verified to make sure nothing was left behind that could be traced back to us. But at the time we viewed sending a recovery team for the bodies as too great a risk for fear that Wolfe would somehow track them back to us."

I pictured the oversized Wolfe driving a car, following a convoy of agents, then had an idle thought wondering what kind of vehicle he would drive. The image of him crammed behind the wheel of a Volkswagon bug popped into my head and in spite of all the emotional turmoil I had to stifle the urge to laugh, which was overtaken by the feeling of sickness again when I thought of him.

"Are you okay?" Ariadne looked at me with a concern that I would have found touching if I trusted her in the slightest. As it was, she spurred my instinct to aim at her if I felt the urge to vomit again.

"I'll be fine." I waved her off. "You didn't come down here to talk to me about my abilities, did you?"

"No," Ariadne replied after a moment's pause. "We came to talk to you about security. Yours."

I felt hollow, a complete lack of emotion. "What about it? Do you want me to leave?"

"No, no." Ariadne shook her head with emphasis. "Now that Wolfe has found our location, though, it changes things. We want to keep you away from the outbuildings and here in the headquarters, where we have the greatest chance to be able to protect you from him."

I wasn't stunned. I wasn't even surprised. But I did feel a clutch of fear at the thought of not being able to see the sky, cloudy though it was, or feel the frigid winter air on my cheeks. Funny, since I'd only just felt it over the last few days, that I was already addicted and unwanting to give it up. "So you don't want me to leave the building…at all? Is that right?"

Ariadne shared an uncertain look with Old Man Winter, who nodded. "Just for the time being," she said, returning her gaze to me. "Until we can resolve this Wolfe situation."

I laughed, that scornful noise I make when I'm not really finding something funny but I want to show my disdain for what's been said. "He's wiped out everything you've sent after him, including your security here on your campus. What, exactly, is going to resolve this 'Wolfe situation'?"

"M-Squad will be returning from special assignment down in the Andes Mountains as soon as we can get in contact with them. Once they return," Ariadne continued, "we have full confidence they'll be able to take Wolfe out of play. Or," she said with another backward look at Old Man Winter, "at least contain him."

"Contain him?" I scoffed again. "The people I've talked to—"

"Meaning Zack," Ariadne interrupted.

I ignored her and continued. "—seem to think that he's one of the strongest metas on the planet. Is that accurate?"

Ariadne exchanged an uncomfortable look with Old Man Winter. And by uncomfortable, I mean on her end. He looked placid as ever. "He is one of the strongest, yes," she said. "But that doesn't mean he can't be stopped."

"That's funny," I said with a calm I didn't feel. "Because Dr. Sessions told me I was a super strong meta, and I can't make much of a dent in him, unless you count when I stuck a pen in his ear."

"A clever strategy, by the way," Ariadne added.

"A desperate one that bought me all of thirty seconds before he reaffirmed his desire to rape and kill me," I raged back at her.

"It bought you enough time to allow us to intervene," she said in a voice that was overly complimentary.

"Allowed him to intervene, you mean." I pointed at Old Man Winter. "Wolfe called you Jotun – a Nordic frost giant." He nodded at me with a ponderous, slow dip of his head but did not speak. "You've faced Wolfe before?" He nodded again. "But you both survived. And Wolfe has been alive for thousands of years?"

Old Man Winter nodded again and broke his silence once more. "He has. A cannier foe there is not; he has survived living on the razor's edge all these years and always among people that are the world's most dangerous. What does it say about him to be able to live millenia in such conditions?"

My heart sank. "That he's dangerous. Worse than anything you can throw at him."

Old Man Winter nodded, once more fixated on my eyes. "In order to protect you, we must keep you in this building. Do you understand?"

Unbidden, a memory of the door of the box closing came to me, and I felt a momentary urge to fight, to argue, to struggle out of my bed and scream at him in defiance. Then the pain in my stomach surged as I moved, and another, hotter emotion came over me, a disgust and humiliation at the thought of Wolfe manhandling me in my room in the dormitory, of his hands all over me, his finger inside my guts, ripping me up...and I almost gagged. "Yes," I said simply, swirling emotions batted to the side.

"Good," Ariadne said with undisguised relief. "I was worried that you might be headstrong and try to resist good sense."

I felt weak, drained. "Glad I could allay your misperceptions." I laid my head on the pillow behind me, not bothering to look at Ariadne or Old Man Winter any longer.

She hesitated. "There will be agents surrounding the medical unit. They're on constant watch, especially after what happened to the agents at your house and the way Wolfe was able to breach security in the dorm. If you need anything – food, books, entertainment – just ask." She smiled, as if she could sense that although I wasn't shooting any venom her way it wasn't because I didn't want to.

She and Old Man Winter left, but only after he gave me another long, hard stare. After they left, Dr. Perugini took a moment to record my vitals, fluffed my pillow with a matronly cluck, and then, with an admonishment to call out if I needed anything, walked to her office and shut the door.

The curtains were up between me and the rest of the patients, and from where I was sitting I could see the backs of agents through the windows, stationed outside the doors of the medical unit, and I heard a healthy cough from behind one of the curtains, telling me there were more behind the partitions. Yet still, I felt alone. Again.

I thought back to what Ariadne had said about expecting a different reaction from me at the thought of being in lockdown. I wondered for just a moment what I must look like to them, how my actions must appear; then I dismissed it and realized I only cared a little. I still didn't trust them. They would protect me now, but for reasons that were their own; reasons that were still unclear to me, but almost certainly involved using me and my powers, whatever they were, for their own ends.

I looked across the unit and found the wall there to be made of reflective metal that allowed me to see a distorted picture of my face. Bruises dotted my cheeks and wrapped around both eyes. There was crusted blood under my nose, and it looked misshapen. My eyes were haunted, the look of someone who had the spirit battered out of them.

The overhead lights went out, dimming the room, and my reflection was shrouded in shadow. It was nighttime; I knew it even though there were no windows.

I heard a door close heavily at the far end of the ward, and it brought me back again to the sound of the box when Mother would slam it shut. "Keep your fingers out of the way," she'd snarl just before she closed it. Then the little clicks followed as she worked the pin in place to lock it. She always shut the little viewing slit last, usually after saying something reassuring or taunting through it, and the light would go out from the world and I'd be alone in the dark, all by myself.

Confinement or Wolfe. I knew which I feared more.

Seventeen

I don't know when I fell asleep but I know that when I did my head was still swirling with thoughts about Wolfe and the fight, if you could call it that. I drifted into a darkness that had little to do with my physical surroundings. I felt myself swallowed in that surreal, faded world that had been present both times I had talked to Reed in my dreams. But this time, somehow, it was different.

The world around me swirled in a sort of rough clarity; as it came into view I recognized the surroundings. Little lights hanging above, soft blue mats on the ground below, and blurred concrete at the edges of my vision gave rise to the realization that I was in my basement. I looked into the corner and sure enough, there it was – the box – peeking out of the darkness, its flat edges visible in the low light of my dream.

"Little doll…" The growling voice sent an involuntary twitch through my body, stiffening my spine and causing me to raise my guard. It did not a whit of good. Wolfe sprung at me from out of the darkness by the box, bounding at me, leaping from all fours. I was paralyzed, unable to move as he crossed the divide between us. I blanched away from the impending hit, throwing all the training Mother had given me right out of the nearest window.

Wolfe sailed toward me, then passed through me as though I were as insubstantial as the air we were breathing. He came to rest without touching the wall, pivoted and came back at me, passing through once more. An angry, perplexed expression darkened his already vicious features, and he bore the look of a man denied his fondest wish. He drew once more to his full height and looked at me with suspicion, keeping his distance and watching me, eyes wary and calculating.

"A dream walker…this is not real…" His voice was low and gravelly, and even though he couldn't touch or hurt me, his words sent a very real chill of fear through my guts in the same place where his finger had ripped into my abdomen.

"What's a dream walker? Is that what this is? What I am?" I put aside my fear, desperate for answers.

He ignored me. "You caught the Wolfe while he's sleeping. Very tricky. You're hiding, sneaking around behind the Directorate's walls, counting on the Jotun to protect you from Wolfe?" His feral smile returned. "Why don't you come out and play? It could be so fun."

"Gee, I wonder why I don't want to face a psychopathic lunatic like you," I snapped at him. Hot anger boiled in me. "You're unhinged."

"Come out and play, little doll." The smile was worse, a nasty, stomach-turning reminder of what he'd tried to do with me; *to* me. "The Wolfe just wants to play."

"Are you stupid? Or are you deaf from where I stabbed you in the ear?" He flinched. I saw it and it gave me a moment of hope. "I'm not coming out. I'm going to stay here, because I have zero desire to be your plaything and die a horrible death after you do God knows what to me."

"You won't die, little doll," his voice rasped. "That wasn't a nice way to play, stabbing Wolfe in the ear. It makes him think about you every time the pain flares. But Wolfe won't kill you, oh no, not yet. Not until they say so, because they want the little doll oh-so-bad."

"Who are *they*…and what do they want me for?" I looked down at him, on all fours, as though he were ready to spring at me again.

"Ah, ah, ah." He shook his head. "I'll tell you if you come out and play."

"I'm not leaving this place," I told him. "Not a chance."

He sighed, a deep, throaty sound. "Wolfe knew you'd say that. But you don't understand...see, Wolfe *has* to have the little doll. Not just for his...masters...but for himself." His eyes looked at me suggestively, leering in a way that would have induced more nausea if I hadn't been transfixed with fear at his words. "So now Wolfe has to be persuasive. Now Wolfe has to convince the little doll to come out of her dollhouse."

My voice cracked. "What...what are you going to do?"

"If Wolfe didn't know better, he would guess that you don't care about people, since you let all those little toy agents get slaughtered at your house." He ran his tongue over his incisors. "But Wolfe thinks maybe you just wanted to play so bad that you didn't think about what would happen to them. But what if Wolfe started playing with others? Would you like that? Would it make you happy or sad to know that other people were getting played with...because of you?" The last bit crossed the realm from suggestive to disgusting as he stood upright and ran a hand down his own chest, raking himself with his claws.

When I said nothing, he continued. "Here's what will happen. Wolfe is going to go out and find a nice family...and he's going to play with them. Mommy, Daddy, little kids. And then he's going to find another. And another. Until the little doll comes out. And if the police try and stop him, well...he'll play with them too, won't he? And we'll just keep going...through this whole rotten city..." His tone turned predatory and savage. "...until the little doll comes out to play."

His grin was surreal now, like the quality of everything else in the dream, but it was growing and expanding, taking over, and I realized I wanted to be away from it, away from him, away from myself. I snapped awake in the medical unit, not even fading back to consciousness like I had with Reed but experiencing a sudden, brutal awakening as though I had missed a step coming down the stairs and tumbled. My breaths were ragged.

I stared into the dark and thought about what Wolfe had said. It had been real, I was sure of it now. I talked to him in my dreams. I was sure of another thing too. His threat to kill others – he *would* carry it out. Carry it out – and love every minute of it. I looked around and saw the curtains still drawn, soft breathing of a few wounded agents coming from the other side of it. Wolfe was going to kill until I came out and faced him. He wouldn't stop until he had me.

And there wasn't a soul that could stop him.

Eighteen

I heard a click at the far end of the medical unit and started, my eyes darting to the door of Dr. Perugini's office where she stood silhouetted in the dimness. She stretched her hands above her head and yawned. "I saw you wake up." She took a long, meandering walk toward me. "Trouble sleeping?"

My hands clutched the sheets, my palms sweaty and sticky. In spite of the warm, comfortable air in the room, I felt a trickle of sweat run down my spine underneath my cloth gown. The bitter taste in my mouth became synonymous with the fear I felt every time I came across Wolfe, and the thudding of my heart was so loud in my ears I was amazed I could hear the doctor. "Yes. Just a…nightmare."

She nodded and stifled another yawn as she snapped on a pair of latex gloves. "Let's check your injury."

"Don't you mean injuries?" I said it with a bitterness that welled up deep inside; a cutting edge of irony that reflected my inner turmoil at the fact that since I left my house I'd been severely beaten twice. Far worse than any punishment Mother had ever levied.

"No," Dr. Perugini said with an odd tone, and reached to the end table behind me, clicking on a lamp and coming back with a mirror. She put it in front of me and I looked at the face within.

There were no visible cuts, marks or bruises. My dark hair and pale skin, my big eyes and pointed nose all looked back at me, a contrast to how I had looked only a few hours before. The only sign that something was different were the bags under my eyes. I looked tired.

"So you see," she said, returning the mirror to the nightstand, "there's only one wound left." She lifted my gown to reveal gauze and bandages on my lower abdomen, around my belly button. "He ripped through the skin and pushed through your peritineum, perforating your intestines." Her brown eyes looked at me, almost as though she were lecturing. "If you were human, it would have taken a surgeon who could work miracles to keep you from dying. All I had to do was give you time to heal yourself."

She peeled back the medical tape securing the bandage to reveal red, scabby tissue beneath, roughly the size of a quarter. She plucked at the pink, sensitive skin around the edges, eliciting a hiss of pain from me. "Be grateful you're alive," she admonished, throwing the bandages in the garbage can and taping a fresh piece of gauze onto the smaller wound, then pushing on my stomach to either side of it. "Any pain here?"

"No." I looked at her hands as she pushed again and this time I cringed, not entirely from the pain. I watched her gloved hands pressing on my skin and had a remembrance, like a flashback in a TV show.

Mom had been sitting on the sofa, not even changed out of her work clothes yet, her dark hair tucked back in a ponytail. She was pretty, I thought, and all I had to compare her to were the actresses on TV. I got my dark hair from her, but her features had always seemed more chiseled than mine, making her look statuesque. Her complexion was darker than mine; not surprising since she did go outside more than I did. Her eyes were green rather than the cool blue of mine.

Her head was resting on the back of the sofa, her eyes lolling a bit, but she focused on me when I approached her. I had in my hand the calculus book that I had been studying from on the kitchen table, my assigned space for working. If I didn't work there, I got in trouble. Needless to say, I only worked in my room when Mom wasn't home.

"Finished your test?" Mom said, looking up at me with indifference. She reached out and took the paper I handed her. She leaned over the end of the couch and pulled the teacher's edition of the book from her bag. She always took them with her so I couldn't cheat by looking up the answers. Nor did we have an internet connection for me to cheat with.

She browsed through it. Her dark eyebrow rose at one point as she chewed on the end of her pen. I stood back, in my sweatpants and t-shirt, the heat of nervous anticipation on my cheeks as I waited to hear the result. She reached the bottom of the paper and looked up at me, still impassive.

"Flawless," she pronounced with a curt nod. "I think you could do a better job of showing your work, however, so keep that in mind next time." She gave me a half smile, the highest mark of affection offered in our house. "You can watch one hour of television, then we do our evening training session."

I let out a squeak of happiness at her pronouncement of TV privileges (I was fourteen, what do you want from me?) followed by the slightest sigh of disappointment at the news of an impending workout. That was the end of her half-smile.

"You think I'm too harsh, but you don't know." Her eyes narrowed and her lips were a thin line. All traces of prettiness vanished in a hard look that drove terror straight through me. "You don't know what's out there."

Her hand pointed toward the front door and I stifled any word of argument I might have given – something along the lines of, "You're right, but only because you won't let me outside…"

She went on. "You can't ever get soft. You can't ever get weak. It's a dangerous world out there, filled with people who want to give nothing but harm to a little girl like you." She stood up and tossed the TV remote on the couch, never looking away as she brushed past me, taking particular care not to touch, and went into her bedroom.

I longed for a hug, affirmation, something. I lowered myself to the couch. All the little words of approval were washed away in the heat of her anger, light as it was. I didn't pay much attention to the TV that night for the hour I watched it, instead thinking about my life and how much I wanted someone to just hold me.

"I expect you'll be up to full strength again within a day," Dr. Perugini spoke, jarring me back to the here and now.

"Good to know," I mouthed more by instinct than from processing the words she'd spoken. She fussed about for a few more minutes, then admonished me to "get some rest" and retreated back to her office, shut the door and turned off the light. I don't know why I wasted my time letting my head get clouded with that stupid memory of Mom when I had Wolfe to think about. His threat.

I had let the doctor distract me for a few minutes while I should have been pondering whether to tell Ariadne and Old Man Winter about my dream. I couldn't blame myself too much, because honestly, I didn't want to think about it. Didn't want to consider the idea that Wolfe might be out there right now, killing people because of me.

I repeated to myself that it was just a dream. Then again. Then five more times. I really wanted this "dream walking" to not be a power but a delusion. I kept repeating it to myself until I fell back to sleep, blissfully uninterrupted by any more horrific visions of Wolfe.

The next morning when I awoke the medical unit was still quiet. I lifted my gown and checked my wound; it was gone. I bent at the waist to sit up and felt no discomfort. I stood, letting my feet touch the cold floor. It didn't bother me.

A hiss came from my left and the door to the unit opened, revealing Ariadne, a key card in one hand, newspaper in the other. "Glad to see you're awake," she said with a perfunctory smile. "We've prepared accommodations in the basement, but first we have to go speak with…" She hesitated.

"Old Man Winter?" I said with a nasty smile in return.

She blanched. "I wouldn't call him that to his face."

"Think he'd get mad at me?" My smile got worse, I could feel it.

"I wouldn't care to find out," she said without further comment. "You should know something."

I froze. "What?"

She threw the newspaper onto the tray by the bed, and underneath the banner was the headline "Family of Five Slaughtered in South Minneapolis". A photo of a home not unlike mine sat underneath the blaring headline. Police tape blocked the entire scene and there were at least a dozen officers in the photograph.

My hands went to my mouth, covering it, pushing the words back in before they could come out. I halted, tried to regain control before speaking. My eyes flew up to Ariadne. Hers were fixed on mine, watching to see my reaction. When I said nothing, she spoke.

"We think it's Wolfe."

Nineteen

I sat across from Old Man Winter in his office, Ariadne standing behind him as always. There was no trace of warmth within these four walls and the day outside looked to be the gloomiest I'd seen thus far. There was a hint of light that told me where the sun had to be, hiding behind a cloud, but the bastard just didn't want to show himself. Ariadne had led me up here after letting me read the article, the gist of which was that another five people were dead because of me.

I clutched the newspaper in my hand and tossed it on Old Man Winter's desk. "Why did you tell me this? Wouldn't it have been more helpful to you if you hid it from me?"

Ariadne shook her head. "You'd find out eventually."

Old Man Winter studied me as he always did. "By telling you, we hope to gain your trust. To let you know that we aren't hiding anything from you; that it is all out in the open."

A roiling torrent of emotion bubbled beneath the calmest exterior I could produce…so probably not all that calm. "Why do you want my trust?"

Ariadne fixated on me. "To let us protect you from Wolfe. We need to keep you safe."

"How can we even be sure it's him?" I hoped it wasn't. I hoped I was wrong, that five more bodies weren't added to the pile of corpses I was responsible for in the week since I'd left home. The number of people dead because of me outweighed the number of people I'd met.

Old Man Winter nudged open a file folder and pulled out a glossy 8x10 photograph, sliding it across the desk to me. I picked it up and stared at it: a photo of a wall. Two bodies were visible at the bottom edge of the shot, a woman and what I thought might have been a little girl; she was almost cropped out of the frame. There were words scrawled on the wall, in a dark crimson that almost looked black: *Waiting for a little doll to come out and play.*

I felt sick all over again, but in a different way.

"There are more," Old Man Winter said in his devastating, quiet timbre. "At least two other houses last night, five more victims. They were not discovered in time to make the morning paper."

A small, plaintive cry of despair escaped my lips. "More?" I croaked. Numbness replaced the sick feeling. "How many more can there be?"

Ariadne looked at me with a pained expression. "Will you let us protect you?"

My mouth was dry. "Who's going to protect all those people out there from Wolfe?"

"We can't protect everybody," Ariadne replied. "All we can do is keep you safe. Will you let us?"

I felt a twinge in my belly where Wolfe had clawed into me. "If I do, how long does this go on?"

"We're trying to make contact with M-Squad, trying to get them back here sooner, but…" Ariadne trailed off.

"Still out of contact," I finished for her, not really hearing my own words. "What are the odds that they can take Wolfe, anyway?"

"I would bet on them," Ariadne said with a slight smile. "They'll sort out Wolfe when they get back. We just need you to endure until they get here. It will get worse before we can make it better."

I leaned back in the chair opposite Old Man Winter. "So I just sit back and let these people die, family by family, to save my own skin?"

An air of silence hung in the office, colder than the air around us. "Would you rather go and face him?" Old Man Winter said. "Would you care to taste what he has in mind for you?"

"They say I'm strong." I spoke fast, words bubbling up from emotional depths, fear and hatred of Wolfe fueling me in equal measure. "Stronger than most metas; and Wolfe is afraid of you – between the two of us, maybe a few others, couldn't we...maybe we could..."

For the first time since I'd known him, Old Man Winter hung his head in obvious defeat. "I cannot win a fight with Wolfe; my earlier efforts at fending him off were purest bluffery. I have not a quarter of the strength I had when last we fought, and he has grown stronger, more canny and more experienced. He would," Old Man Winter said with resignation, "destroy me in mere moments, and you shortly thereafter, along with any other metas we brought along." His head came up, and the cold blue eyes held an aura of sadness.

Ariadne spoke, her words coming almost as low as his. "You are the strongest meta left on the campus at present. Only one other is even close. Not enough to take Wolfe."

"No," he said, shaking his head again, "M-Squad has all the strength of the Directorate and it is in them that our hope lies."

"So we just sit back, hide, and watch as he kills three or four families a night until M-Squad comes back?" My voice was raw. I thought back to my encounters with Wolfe and wondered again if there was any way I could beat him myself. I thought about the pen in his ear and wondered at any other weak points he might have; eyes, mouth...his bones felt unbreakable, but with enough force they could surely be destroyed. The only question would be what could deliver enough force. "There has to be a way to beat him."

"Would you suggest shooting him?" Ariadne asked.

"No," I said with a shake of the head. "Guns don't even

break the skin. The tranquilizer darts, though. Maybe if we loaded him up with those darts…"

"Based on what we've seen, one of his powers seems to be to adapt to attacks – the shock cannon that Kurt hit him with was less effective each successive time it was used, to the point where he shrugged it off when he attacked us here." She cast a sidelong glance at Old Man Winter. "We suspect his resistance to bullets is something that has developed over time; it's doubtful that the darts or the toxin would be as effective this time around."

"He has always been uncannily adaptable to changing situations," Old Man Winter said, "and has lived through battles that have killed lesser metas by the hundreds. There is a reason that Wolfe and his brothers have lived for thousands of years."

"There has to be a way to beat him," I said with urgency. "Something. Some weapon in your arsenal that you haven't tried yet, like that shock cannon…something that can just buy us a few minutes."

"I'm sorry," Ariadne said, voice gentle. "There's nothing. We've bluffed him well enough that he seems to be steering well clear of the Directorate, but until M-Squad returns, it is only a bluff. We need to keep you here, protect you, until we can work out this situation. It's the only course we have available."

My voice cracked. "Unless I give myself up."

"Ridiculous," Ariadne replied. "You know what he would do to you. Do you really want to go through that?"

"No," I answered. "But neither do I want to keep sacrificing others, watching bodies pile up and families get destroyed because I'm too scared to face Wolfe."

"Give us a little more time," Ariadne said in a pleading tone. "Let us get M-Squad back. Once they're here, we can take care of Wolfe."

I put my hands in front of my face and started doing the mental arithmetic. Two dead in the parking lot outside the grocery store. Eight at my house when I wanted to face Wolfe the first time. Eight more when he attacked the Directorate campus. Ten last night, none of whom I'd even met. Almost thirty dead at the hands of Wolfe, every single one of them because they stood between me and that maniac. How many would it take? What if I left town? Like Zack said, he might eventually find me, but how many people would he kill in the interim? Hundreds? Thousands? Would he eventually just burn the city to the ground?

The fear choked me again. I wasn't as afraid of dying as I was of what Wolfe was going to do to me first. I had caught a sample of his idea of play and the thought of uninterrupted time with him doing what he liked was enough to make me sick again. He would violate me in ways that I couldn't imagine, based on my limited experience in the world and with men. In a way, my naïveté probably spared me from being even more fearful. Or maybe the fear of the unknown made it worse.

I looked back to Ariadne and Old Man Winter, who were looking at me, waiting for a response. I wanted to be brave. Part of me wanted to fight him again, to knock him down, to make him fear me the way I feared him.

But my hands felt weak. They shook. I couldn't beat him, I knew that. I didn't want him to touch me, didn't want to smell his disgusting, rotten breath or feel his claws caressing my skin and drawing blood, didn't want to feel him rubbing and pushing against me again. I choked on my cowardice and justified it in my head – I didn't want to be near him again. Ever.

All I wanted was to go home, back to the simple world of Mom, and when I was bad, the box. Nobody but me got hurt there. Nobody died.

But Mom was gone. My house was forfeit; it was Wolfe's domain now, he owned it, and every thought I had of it from now on would be tainted by the memory of how he beat me, broke me in that basement in a way my mother and the box never had. I had nothing left but the Directorate, and no one to trust but these two people that I didn't even know.

I looked from Old Man Winter to Ariadne, each in turn. Winter was brooding and quiet while Ariadne was waiting with patient expectation. I choked on my words, but finally they came out, filling my ears with the sound of my cowardice, drawing a nod from Winter and a smile from Ariadne.

"You win."

Twenty

Two days and twenty-eight dead bodies later, I wished I hadn't listened to my fear. I had been stewing in a basement room of Headquarters, walls made of reinforced concrete and plated with steel or some other metal that didn't bend when I punched it out of fury or frustration or sheer pitying despair. I punched it a lot.

Ariadne had done everything in her power to make me comfortable in my oversized room. I had my own bathroom, they'd brought in a bed from one of the dormitories that felt like it was cushioned with air – not that I'd been sleeping, but I lay down on it a lot while I watched the news.

They'd brought me a big TV and it was tied in to all the networks. I flipped back and forth between three different local channels and the national news stations depending on who was on commercial. Having never been able to watch TV for more than an hour a day, news was never on my to-watch list. I always caught a smattering over Mom's shoulder at night while I studied at the table, but I much preferred sitcoms and dramas over news.

I found myself glued to the goings-on. One network proclaimed: "Minneapolis: City Under Siege" while another network decried that Minneapolis was "In the Grip of Terror." The third was speculating on the source of the violence and assigning blame politically.

The local stations were somewhat less objective as the anchors seemed to be in fear for their lives. It was hard not to feel for them the same way I'd feel for characters on the TV shows I watched – sitcoms had the ability to bring me to tears, which I always hid from Mom. She would roll her eyes and make snide comments about "weakness."

As I watched the news hour after hour, as the days ticked by, I felt nothing but weak. I wished I'd told Ariadne and Old Man Winter to stick their offer of safety in a warm and uncomfortable place. I stared at the walls as the news showed photos of the latest victims, trying to avoid the looks on the faces of the family in the picture. They were all smiling, but it felt like they were silently accusing me of dooming them to death. This one was a family with a dark haired father, a blond haired mother and two little blond girls. All staring at the photographer with happy smiles on their faces.

Now dead. Because of me. Because of my cowardice.

The door slid open and the agent outside stuck his head in. "Visitor, miss." He said it without a wasted syllable or any emotion. After two days and a half dozen such messages, I was beginning to suspect that the agents assigned to guard me had very clear memories of their fellows who died at my house, and what they had died for. There was not a drop of the milk of human kindness in any of the men I had interacted with while in this place. The only friendly face was Ariadne's, and she had dropped in for conversations twice now – ones which I had kept civil by virtue of not wanting them to end prematurely.

After twelve years alone and one week in the company of others, I found myself not wanting to go back to alone.

I was sitting on the bed, t-shirt and pajama pants on, in violation at last of Mom's fourth rule, the only one that I had been following lately, the one that demanded I remain fully dressed, down to my gloves and shoes at all times, ready to move. (When she wasn't home I frequently took my shoes and my gloves off, among other things, which led to punishments if I wasn't quick enough on the days she'd arrive unexpectedly early).

I had been enjoying the feel of the soft bed against my skin, something in great contrast to the marked discomfort I felt on the inside from what I was watching. Self-consciousness came over me as I realized I wasn't dressed for visitors, then tried not to care.

I jumped to my feet as the door slid open again to admit a familiar face. Zack walked in wearing a leather jacket, his hair tousled, and gave me a smile. I breathed a sigh of relief; I hadn't seen him since Wolfe attacked the Directorate. Then I felt a stir of embarrassment for my attire; I would have preferred to greet him in something more presentable. Or presentable at all, really. I stood in place, ummoving, the bed between us. His arm was immobilized in a sling and his face was flecked with cuts. A bandage still covered his nose but otherwise he looked fine.

"How are you holding up?" he asked after he'd seated himself at the table in the corner of the room. I sat across from him, reminded of the last time we had talked like this, in the cafeteria a few days earlier.

"Me?" I asked, breaking through the dark clouds of emotion. "I'm fine, physically. You still look wrecked, though."

He raised an eyebrow. "Physically, huh? Yeah, I look pretty rough. Us humans don't heal as quick as you metas. I wasn't asking about how you're doing physically, I can see you're fine." He sat back and winced as he bumped the back of the chair with his elbow. "How are you holding up...in other areas?"

"You mean emotionally?" Two days of beating the hell out of myself for my cowardice left me without the strength to lie. "I feel like crap. Lower than low." My voice came out so matter-of-factly, Zack blinked in disbelief. "I feel like I've sacrificed the lives of everyone who's died so I can save my own ass."

His disbelieving expression spread from a cocked eyebrow to the downturned corners of his mouth. "Do you think you can beat him?"

"No, I don't think I can beat him." The sterile air of the room washed through my nose as I took a breath. "I don't think I can even come close."

"Then why try?" He looked at me with incredulity. "You made the smart play. Wolfe's a psycho killer; he's lived way longer than any of us; he'll outlive us all unless M-Squad can kill him. You're crazy if you don't let us protect you."

"How long?" I asked, the emotion breaking into my voice. "How long do I keep watching them report person after person dead? How long can I hide behind you guys? Don't you think at some point Wolfe will get tired of slaughtering innocent people and come back here for another round?" I stared at my hands, pressed palm down on the cold surface of the metal table. Everything in this place had the feel of sterility, of having never been lived in.

"Old Man Winter doesn't think that'll happen."

"Then Old Man Winter's crazy." I pulled my hands up and folded them. "Wolfe loves to kill and he loves pain. He'll come back here sooner or later, when he gets tired of the slaughter. He'll go through the dormitory building before you drive him off again, or try to get through HQ – he'll find me eventually, and all that's going to be different is how many people he kills between now and that day." The quiet certitude of that thought filled me, and I watched Zack's expression deteriorate as he pondered it.

"It's not gonna happen like that. M-Squad is coming back. You've never met them: they are the toughest metas you can imagine. They'll set a trap for Wolfe and they'll punch his ticket. That's if the Minneapolis cops don't get him first."

"He'll go through them like a boat through water."

"Yeah, in ones and twos – but they'll be deploying in big numbers and call in state and FBI for a case like this." Zack's eyes were animated. "My degree is in criminal justice. Once they get a taste of him, they may even call in the National Guard. Mark my words, this town's about to get too hot for Wolfe. He'll either bail or—"

"Decide it's not worth the trouble waging a campaign of

terror and turn right back to attacking the Directorate." I stared him down. "And we're back to the same place – how many die before he gets me?"

Zack almost seemed to retreat. "He's not some invincible god creature. He's just damned strong and canny." Suspicion clouded his features. "You almost sound like you've given up. You eager to get raped to death by him?"

"That's so stupid I'm not going to dignify it with a response," I shot back. "But he seems unstoppable! So the alternatives are run and hide somewhere else – which lets him slaughter a whole bunch more people so I can get away or keep hiding here, which again leads to the slaughter of more people and eventually me. Or I could just get it over with now."

My fingers crept up to my face, lending it support. I was more tired than I was willing to acknowledge. "The idea of him slaughtering more people is wearing on me. It's wearing on my mind. My conscience. What did any of them do to deserve this?"

"Deserve doesn't have much to do with it," Zack said in a gentle tone. "What did you do to deserve having this psycho want to gut you?"

I paused before answering, and a steady flash of images rolled before my eyes, of all the times I'd ended up in the box, all the little crimes I'd perpetrated, all the little acts of defiance against Mom. All the punishments, all the times I was bad. "I don't know," I mumbled, lying.

"Listen…" He paused. "Old Man Winter is sending me to South America with a couple other guys to track down M-Squad. Figure I'm going to be gone for a few days because we don't know exactly where they are. While I'm gone…" He paused again and his eyes bored into mine. "Please don't do anything crazy, like go after Wolfe." He thought for a second and amended, "Again."

I sat very still, fighting not to make a sound. When I answered him, it was as bold a lie as I thought I could get away with. "I don't think they'd let me out at this point."

His voice hinted that his disbelief at my last answer had carried over to this one. "I don't think you're the sort to ask permission after you've made a decision. Which is why I'm asking you..." A hint of pleading entered his tone. "Please let me get M-Squad. Just hold on until I get back."

The earlier picture of the family from the news, their accusing eyes, shot through me. "People are dying."

"I know." He nodded and bowed his head in a sort of solemnity. "And I really, really don't want you to be one of them. Old Man Winter says there's a reason...something about you had Wolfe's employer pull out all the stops and send him instead of anybody else. He says it means you're important...maybe even vital...to what's going to happen in the future."

At that moment I would have happily given up everything I had, including my so-called powers, whatever they might be, in exchange for a destiny that included me living a normal life where I never had to worry about people dying for me. Maybe a boyfriend, eventually a husband, a house I could leave at will, a job, friends...minor things. "I could stand to be a little less important at this point," I said with muted interest. I was so down I didn't even care much what that meant.

"I don't want to see you get killed." Zack lowered his head to try and meet my eyes. I didn't look away from him, but I didn't have much energy left. "You've had a rough life so far, and I'd hate to see you get taken out before you had a chance to actually live it."

"Live it?" I echoed. "How?"

"Have you ever been to a movie in the theater?" He stared back at me, slight smile lightening his face. "Or been out to a restaurant and then to a club? Done any dancing? Been to a concert? Gone to the mall? Comedy show? Theater? Been to Valley Fair?" I shook my head after each question, remembering commercials I'd seen, things I'd put on a list in a diary that had been under my bed for years, something I'd outgrown.

Actually, something I'd put aside because Mom thought it was too close to breaking rule #5: no talking about the outside world. "No," I said.

"They're all things I think you'd enjoy," he went on. "I need you to hang on…just a little longer…til I get M-Squad, and they take care of Wolfe." He said it with a reassuring smile. I could feel his confidence and I knew he believed to his depths that M-Squad could take Wolfe. I was less sure, but it didn't matter. He believed it totally. "Will you promise me you'll wait?"

I didn't know what to say. I felt the pressure of his eyes on me, so calm and reassuring, looking at me in a way I had rarely seen. "I…I…" I stuttered.

Caring. That's what his eyes were. And I realized again how good looking he was. And older. And I tried to keep in mind that he was spying for Ariadne and Old Man Winter, but that thought faded when I looked into his deep brown eyes. "I…I promise."

"Attagirl." He stood, extending a hand to help me up. I humored him and took it, feeling a little dazed. I kept focused on him and watched his eyes swim for a moment, and he let go of my hand. "I should…uh…get going." He took a step and seemed to trip, then cast a look back at me to see if I noticed. "Felt a little lightheaded there for a second." His smile turned to a grin. "Must be the effect of being around you." He walked to the door and knocked on it, then left when it slid open, sending me back one last smile.

I groaned when he left, mostly from the last cheesy line he'd said, but also from the fact that he'd extracted the promise from me that he had. My fingers tingled with pleasure from the feel of his touch on my hand and left me wondering about all the things in the world that I'd never experienced – but less about the ones he had mentioned…and more about the ones he hadn't.

Twenty-one

Three more days, one hundred and thirty-two more dead. I was well past the point of sick and into the realm of deathly numb, if such a thing existed. If I had any doubt that I was the world's worst person, it was dissolved when some unnamed individual slid a note under my door that I found first thing in the morning. I didn't bother to ask the guards how it got there. It read:

People are dying by the hundreds and you're hiding. If he comes back here, you won't find much help from any of us because everyone here pretty much hates you and we're all rooting for him to turn you inside out.

Ariadne hadn't stopped by in several days and the guards hadn't initiated any conversations, so my only human contact was when a cafeteria worker brought me meals three times per day. It was always the same person, a middle-aged woman who didn't have anything to say. At all. I caught her scowling at me when she thought I wasn't looking. Based on her attitude, I had to guess the letter was on target.

The crisis in Minneapolis had gotten so bad that there were police and SWAT teams on constant call. Helicopters circled, watching for any sign. Wolfe had progressed from only slaughtering people in their homes to killing people in public places as he moved between potential victims – he had been caught on several automated cameras. When four houses in a row in one of the western suburbs was hit it started a louder clamor; previously Wolfe had restricted himself to working in Minneapolis proper.

Since then he had jumped around, but the police always

seemed to be a couple steps behind him, at least according to the news. Hundreds of witnesses reported seeing him, even just a flash in passing, and the police were overwhelmed because at the slightest hint of a noise people were calling 911 for help; as a result, instances of violent crime were up 142% (again, according to the news) and tons more were going unnoticed. As one reporter put it, "It's a good time to get away with murder in Minneapolis because, amidst all the other bodies, who's going to investigate one more?"

All my fault. Every last one of them.

I was still glued to the TV, watching every update, every bit of breaking news that really wasn't breaking, every police press conference, every release of another victim's name. I felt more powerless than at any time prior in my life, worse than any occasion I'd been locked away. When I was prisoner in my own home I never had to worry my actions would cause harm to anyone or anything – except maybe Mom's feelings, if she had any.

I was waiting, hoping to hear that M-Squad had returned or that Wolfe had been run over by a garbage truck (maybe that would kill him) or anything – anything to break the twenty-four hour press of guilt.

And then I did.

"Breaking news," I heard an anchorperson say for the one millionth time in the last few days. I was lying on the floor. It wasn't as soft as the bed but I didn't feel like I deserved the bed right now. "We go live now to Winston Haines, who is in a chopper above Southdale Mall, where Edina police have cornered the suspect in the slayings that have gripped the Twin Cities in a wave of terror."

I stood and moved closer to the TV. The angle changed to look down on a parking lot, where a lone figure raced across the pavement. My heart stopped, along with my breath.

It was Wolfe.

I watched as he hurdled a car, running flat out from three police cruisers and a SWAT van that were behind him. Two more cruisers cut him off and boxed him in. Cops opened doors and I saw them fire right away, not even bothering to say anything. It was a smart move on their part, but I had to wonder if it would be enough.

Wolfe went down to a knee under the sheer volume of gunfire. The reporter was blathering on about civil rights but I silently cheered the cops on, hoping that they would put him down like the rabid dog he was.

And maybe it would be over. And I could get out of here. And go…anywhere else. Somewhere that I wouldn't have to think about any of this.

The SWAT van popped open and black-suited team members swarmed toward Wolfe, who was now on all fours, and a moment of silence prevailed as the reporter shut up. They surrounded him and I hoped that maybe the bullets they had shot him with had more power than the shotgun rounds I'd seen him shrug off. They pointed their guns at him point blank, and then one of them stepped in, handcuffs at the ready, going slow, amazed that Wolfe was still alive and moving after the hail of bullets that had been thrown at him.

As he started to reach for Wolfe's hand to place the cuffs on, I flinched away. It was an involuntary response born of the realization that something terrible was about to happen. When I blinked my eyes open a second later, it was already done. Wolfe was in motion, his claws raking through body armor, sending cops flying through the air just as he had when he assaulted the Directorate.

They didn't shift the camera away from the scene, which surprised me, especially when the blood started to flow. Wolfe swept through the SWAT team in less than ten seconds, and their

Kevlar vests and riot helmets did nothing to stop his slashes and punches.

When he was finished with the SWAT team, he started on the cops from the cars that had surrounded him. The first few kept shooting, dodging him in futile efforts to escape his grasp. He used his teeth when he got hold of them. The last few ran, each in a different direction, and the camera followed him as he bounded after them. I didn't watch nature programs very often, but I'd seen lions take down wounded gazelles, and it was disgusting to watch.

The reporter provided commentary on the horrors of what we were seeing as Wolfe finished the last police officer with a rough decapitation, holding the man's head up in the air, facing toward the helicopter. He then pointed right at the camera, and it zoomed in to the point where every detail of his horrible face was visible, his teeth, his black eyes and even the blood dripping from his claws as he pointed.

At me. I could feel it. He was pointing at me. He hoped I was watching. Maybe he *knew* I was watching.

He mouthed words. "We don't know quite what he's saying..." The reporter's voice was sheer astonishment. But he was wrong. I knew exactly what he was saying. And I didn't even have to be that good at reading lips to figure it out; just had to have heard the repetitive taunting from him, with that same sadistic look, the one that I knew contained not one ounce of insincerity.

"Little doll...come out and play."

Twenty-two

Wolfe bolted into the mall at the approach of another half dozen cop cars; probably not because he couldn't take them all out and then some, but because he had other things on his agenda. The news reported later that he'd cut his way through the patrons of the stores, leaving another thirty or so dead, a few others wounded before he bolted out an exit and disappeared.

At this point I was ill enough that I flipped off the TV. Watching wasn't helping. A reminder that I'd had a hand in the deaths of another sixty or more people, people who had families, parents, kids – that didn't help me at all. It didn't help me want to keep my promise to Zack, anyway.

I stared at the stainless steel walls for the next hour. I resolved not the smash the TV to pieces, no matter how much I wanted to vent my frustration. I went to the bathroom and took a long, hot shower, but not as long as I wanted because I kept thinking about all the people dead right now that wouldn't ever again get to experience the simple pleasure of something as basic as a hot shower on a cold day. Or shopping malls. Or theaters…or anything that Zack had listed off. Ever again.

Or a hug from someone who loved them.

I had been ready to turn off the water and get out when I started shaking with emotion at that thought. I heard someone say once that it wasn't possible to miss what you never had. But if that was true, why did I want someone to love me, to hold me, just once?

It took me almost twenty minutes to compose myself, and when I stepped out my dinner was waiting for me, along with an unpleasant surprise.

"I brought your food," Kurt Hannegan said with a sneer. "No one else wanted anything to do with you." He had been almost to the door to leave and had turned back just to toss the shot at me.

"I'm not hungry."

"I guess it's hard to work up an appetite when all you do is sit by while people die because of you." He paused at the door for a beat, then turned to knock on it so the guard would let him out.

"Wait," I called to him. My voice must have sounded as lifeless to him as it did to me, because he listened.

"What?" The air of impatience surrounded him as if, insult now delivered, he couldn't wait to get away from me.

"I don't want anybody to die," I said in a voice that sounded smaller to me than I could have imagined when I formed the words.

"It's a little late for that now," he snarled. "Hell, it was too late the day after you goaded Old Man Winter into sending us back to your house."

"I need your help," I said to him.

He laughed. "You've had my help before and all it got was a bunch of my buddies dead—"

"I want to go to Wolfe. Myself." He raised a stunned eyebrow. "I don't want anybody else to die. I need to get out of here so I can go to Wolfe; so I can end this." I held up my hands at my sides. "So I can give him what he wants."

Hannegan hesitated, regarding me with suspicion. "You playing games with me?"

"No," I said, returning to the lifeless voice. "I just want this to be over."

"Yeah," he said, suddenly incensed, "and get my ass fired for helping you commit suicide." His eyes narrowed. "But I tell you what…your guard changes at seven A.M. If someone was to try and escape an hour before that, at six, especially if they were super strong, they could sweep through the guards – without hurting anybody seriously," he said with emphasis, "and there might be a few minutes when the cameras were off. If you went west, past the cafeteria and across the field toward the woods, there's a road behind the wall of the campus. A meta could clear it with a jump, easy."

"And what would I find there?" I was hollow, just waiting to see what he had in mind.

"Maybe nothing. Maybe a ride." He turned back to the door. "I wouldn't want to be accused of helping you."

"You're not," I said in a rasp.

He knocked on the door and left without further comment. After he was gone, I stared at the blank TV screen for a while. Decision made. You know what finally did it? What finally pushed it over the top? I saw at least one of the dead cops was a woman. She looked to be of an age where she might have a little girl. A little girl whose mom wouldn't come home tonight.

Sounds familiar.

I watched TV to kill the time without falling asleep. I found now that the decision was made, all the weariness of the last few days was creeping in, ready to overtake me. But I couldn't let it, not yet. They hadn't left me an alarm clock and I didn't trust myself not to sleep through this, or I would have tried to contact Wolfe in my dreams. I asked the guard at the door for some coffee. He sneered, made a sarcastic comment about how he wasn't my serving wench, and let me know he'd have someone else deal with it.

I couldn't wait to punch him in the face.

I'd never passed slower hours, not even in the box, without any visual or auditory stimuli but those I made myself. Every news report that rehashed the incident at the mall and all the new deaths seemed elongated, stretching into infinity. The metal hands of the clock that hung in my room moved as though they weighed tons rather than grams.

The last five minutes were the worst. I would follow the plan Kurt laid out. Even though I didn't trust him, I suspected he wouldn't have any problem taking me to die, especially if he could get away with it.

With two minutes left, I stared back at the news. The timing was perfect: they were just beginning a montage of pictures of all the people who had died so far in this insanity. I watched their faces scroll by, some smiling and innocent – the children, mostly – some staid and serious, caught in candid shots. I would have wept, but my resolve was hardened. Soon enough, there wouldn't be any more.

I walked to the door at six, knocked on the steel and waited for it to slide open. When it did, the same guy that had told me that he wasn't my serving wench became my bitch instead, and I battered him against the opposite wall with a single punch. Not bad, considering he was at least a hundred pounds heavier than me.

Three more guards flooded the hallway. I pulled the gun from the first and heaved it at the farthest guy, and my enhanced dexterity scored a perfect hit; the butt of the shotgun clipped him in the jaw. I had seen people get knocked out before, but this time it was like slow motion; his eyes fluttered, he looked woozy for a second, then he dropped to his knees and flopped facedown.

I grabbed the closest guy to me as he went for his radio and yanked him forward, pulling him off balance with the ease of uprooting a small plant. I landed a hammerfist on the back of his head and he went down. I surged forward with a front kick, catching the last guy in the corridor in the stomach, knocking the wind out of him. I followed up with a punch that broke his jaw as well as knocked him out, giving the Directorate guards yet another reason to hate me. There were so many.

After the last one hit the floor, I looked down the steel-plated corridor. It stretched about a hundred feet in either direction, and there was no sound or movement. Most of the Directorate staff were out for the night, so this building was likely much quieter than, say, the dormitory building where all the metas and on-campus staff lived. Nonetheless, I crept quietly up the stairs to the first floor, where, without even leaving the stairwell, I found an exit door.

I studied it in a rush, making sure it wasn't an emergency exit that would set off a fire alarm. It didn't appear to be, so I pushed through the crossbar and opened it, sprinting out into the snow. I was back in my turtleneck, coat and gloves...the only thing I was missing was a ridiculous hat to keep my head warm. And I was headed home.

I ran across the snow, heading toward the woods. I passed the dormitory building, giving it a wide berth, snow up to my knees but still moving fast, when the alarm klaxons began howling. They might have found my handiwork in the basement. All those guards beaten senseless.

I didn't spare a thought for it, just ran faster. I was having to lift my legs high to clear the snow, but I was amazed at how fast I was moving. I went several hundred yards through two feet of snow in seconds. I reached the tree line and kept moving, trusting my reflexes to keep me from getting clotheslined by a low-hanging branch or plowing into a tree trunk.

Darkness appeared in front of me and I realized it was the wall. It stretched a good ten feet up and was made of solid block.

And I cleared it in a jump.

I landed on the other side with an inelegant roll, brushing off the snow as I got to my feet. I heard slow clapping coming from in front of me. Lit by the beams of headlights, Kurt Hannegan stood in front of his car. "Very nice. Now can we get out of here?"

I followed him, getting into the passenger side and shutting the door. He gunned the gas, wheels slipping on the wet pavement.

"Where to?" he asked, hands gripping the wheel and his jaw clenched.

"Just drive me to my house," I told him, brushing the snow off myself. He shot me an angry look as he watched it land on the upholstery. "I have to let Wolfe know where to find me."

"Do it after I'm gone," he said with a scowl.

"Fine," I lied. "I'm going to sleep until we get there."

"Don't know why you're bothering," he shot back. "You'll be getting plenty of that soon."

I didn't respond to his dig, instead leaning back in the seat, resting my head against the side of the car, close to the window. The steady thrum of the tires against the road gave off perfect white noise, and the motion of the vehicle rocked me to sleep.

Darkness encompassed me, enshrouded me, took me away from the road and the headlights and that asshole Hannegan, and deposited me right where I wanted to be. Blackness surrounded me, swirled me into its vortex, and then, in the distance, I saw a spot. Burrowing through the dark, it got clearer and clearer, coalescing into a shape – like a man, but with black eyes, horrific teeth and a face that gave me nothing but fear. He drew closer and closer, a smile lighting his terrible features. A smile that broadened when I spoke.

"Wolfe…it's time to play."

Twenty-three

I woke up, intentionally, a few minutes later to find myself rolling through the streets of my neighborhood. We'd left behind the wide open farmland, the stretches of suburbs and freeway, and entered the densely packed blocks of houses that had only a few feet between them. I lifted my head to find Hannegan looking around in all directions, as if he were expecting Wolfe to ambush.

"I don't think he's here yet," I said with a hint of amusement. Not sure where that came from. Gallows humor, I assume.

"I don't care; I'm not hanging around." He kept up his searching pattern. "You may be ready to die but I'm not."

"I'm not really ready to die," I said. "But neither are any of the people he's killing to get to me."

Hannegan grunted in acknowledgment, but did it so neutrally I wondered if he'd heard a word of what I said. He came to a stop at the end of a driveway and I looked up at the house. Unlike last time, I was sure it was mine. I opened the door and pondered making a sarcastic comment to him or lingering for a moment, but I realized I was more scared of what was coming than vindictive about what had happened in the past.

I wordlessly shut the door and I watched him swallow heavily, the sort of action that might make a gulping sound had I been in the car to hear it. He looked at me with hollow eyes and I could see his fear at the thought of facing Wolfe. He looked away and stomped the accelerator, slinging muddied slush on me as he sped away.

I sat there, freezing, in disbelief for a moment, sopping wet. "Screw it," I said and pulled my gloves off, throwing them into the gutter. I pulled my jacket off, also soaked, and tossed it on the ground. I took a couple steps toward my front door and faltered.

He probably wasn't in there yet. Probably. I found myself in no great hurry to find out. He was either here or on his way.

The chill wind combined with the lingering wetness of Kurt's spinout caused a frigid feeling that was eating into my bones. Still, I stopped at the edge of the driveway and scooped up a handful of snow. I felt the cold of it, the dull feeling of numbness that started radiating through my palm after I held it against my bare skin for a few moments. I couldn't have imagined two weeks ago that everything would end up like this.

I thought again about Zack and I wondered where he was, if he was still in South America. It didn't matter; I had no faith that M-Squad could take on Wolfe and win. I thought about his list of things, the things that I never got to do. That I would never get to do. Then I thought about the other list, the one I made after he left that night. Things he didn't mention, like having a first date…getting my first kiss…

I felt tears stinging at the corners of my eyes and I looked back to the house where I'd spent every hour and every day of my remembered life up until a week ago. Those four walls enclosed my life like a grave, and they would likely end up being my tomb, the place where my body would lie, maybe forever.

The hell of it was, with Mom missing, there really wasn't anybody else who'd care I was gone – care about me, the real me, not the supposedly super-powerful meta that everyone was chasing. Who's so powerful she can't even save herself.

I looked up past the trees that stretched into the sky. They'd been there for decades, growing in the ground here on this street. Clouds covered the sun, just as they had every day since I ran out the front door. I walked, slow, shuffling steps, each one an act of pure will, as I made my way to the door. I was going to die without ever even seeing the sun.

I remembered a few days before, when Wolfe first threatened to do what he'd done to this city. I recalled being so sure that there was not a soul that could stop him, but truthfully there was all along. The problem with being self-centered, as we humans are, is that sometimes we miss the obvious solutions when the effect on us is less than desirable. There was a person who could stop Wolfe. And it was me. I could stop him. And all I had to do was give him what he wanted most. And what I wanted least.

My hand felt the cold metal of the doorknob as I turned it, opening the porch door. I stepped inside and felt it slam shut behind me. I sat there in the semi-darkness, just breathing for a moment before I took my next step forward and entered the front door. I looked down, expecting to see the dead agent's body that had been left here last time, but it was gone. There wasn't a sound in the house, but outside I could hear a far-off police siren, probably answering the call of another person worried about Wolfe slaughtering them.

I looked around the living room as I shut the door behind me. It was still in scattered disarray from the battles it had seen in recent days. Wasn't your life supposed to flash before your eyes before you die? Not that I had a life; just a thin, cardboard cutout version of reality that involved me waking up every day, eating breakfast, reading books, working out and, if I was good, sitting on the couch that was upturned in front of me and watching an hour of TV before I went to bed at night.

It wasn't a life. My entire existence was circumscribed by the same walls I was looking at now, the walls of this house, and when I was bad, the walls of the box.

The box. That damned box.

I slipped down the stairs to the basement, leaving the wreckage of the living room behind me, replete with the smell of gore. The lights were still hanging overhead, the mats still bloody where Zack and I had left our contribution from the fight with

Wolfe. I stepped over them and made my way to the corner to look at it.

It didn't matter if I grew ten feet taller, I would still look at it as a huge, metal, imposing figure. The side that swung open hung off its hinges, moved from where I left it. The last time…I tried to put the hinges back together, tried to set it right again, to make it look like it wasn't broken. It stood open, the darkness inside a silent reminder of days spent within.

I wish there was some brave, exciting reason why I tried to fix it, but the truth is that as irrational as it sounds, I feared Mom's reaction when she saw I'd broken out. It was the act of a scared little girl that vainly hoped her mother wouldn't realize that when she left the house, I was locked in a metal sarcophagus and when she got back, I was sleeping in my own bed and sitting on my own couch and going about my life unfettered by the metal prison she'd confined me to before she left.

Of course, she never came back, so it didn't matter. I wondered what Mom would say when she found out what happened to me. If she found out. I wondered if Wolfe had caught up with her, as well. Mom was a fighter; way better than me. If he did, I bet she hurt him before the end. The thought of the pen sticking out of his ear, blood trailing down his face, came back to me, along with the thought of tranquilizer darts and the knife I had buried in him last time I was here. Yeah. Mom would have given him hell.

"Little doll," I heard from behind me, turning to face the staircase. He strolled down, an idle man with all the time in the world. His nose was sniffing, as if he were savoring the meal he was about to eat. He paused at the last step. "So nice of you to call on Wolfe. I was beginning to question how many people I was going to have to kill before you'd pay attention…of course," he admitted with a broad grin, worthy of his name, "Wolfe can't take credit for all the kills the news has been giving to him…someone else has joined in on Wolfe's good times…"

"Who?" A brief spark of interest crossed my mind as my brain scrambled for ways to avoid the fate I knew was moments away.

A shrug from the beast. "Wolfe doesn't know. Wolfe doesn't care." A grin. "Wolfe cares about you, little doll. Wolfe knows from the little samples how good you taste…now he wants the full course." He paused and wagged his finger at me. "Wolfe thinks you know that you can't beat him. But before we start, he wants to hear you promise you won't try."

An involuntary shudder passed through me and I gave my full effort to blotting out thoughts of what was about to happen. "I can't beat you," I admitted. "And if I kept running, I believe you will keep killing forever; everyone you could – men, women and children. It would never get better. It would be my fault. And that realization would sap every ounce of joy from my life – or what passes for my life – forever."

He took another step closer. "Wise, for one so young, to know the Wolfe so well. Wolfe is amazed that one so cut off all her life can feel connected to this world…but it matters not." He swept closer in one swift movement and I didn't resist as he closed his hand around my neck. "Wolfe is going to hurt you now…and this will go on for quite some time…until you can't resist even if you want to…and then, when you can't move, but you can still feel…then we'll start the real fun…"

He slammed me against the wall and it felt like the world ended. My ears rang as though someone had set off the planet's worst rock band in them, and it hurt like hell. My brain was swimming and for a moment the world spun upside down and then righted itself. Wolfe was still staring back at me with those black, lifeless eyes, like I was an insect he was studying. "I don't want you to move for your own good, little doll…dolls shouldn't move themselves when Wolfe plays with them…so this is for your own good…"

He reached back for a windup and threw me across the room and headfirst into the concrete. I don't know for sure that it fractured my skull, but the gawdawful cracking noise told me that either my bones or the wall had given. Blood covered my face, trickling over my eyes. I could only feel it, not see it, because my eyelids had snapped shut. He grabbed hold of me again and hauled me into the air. My hands twitched at my side.

"Wolfe wouldn't be doing this if you hadn't hurt him. He would have handed you over to his masters, like they wanted, all safe and sound, but you had to hurt the Wolfe…not once, not twice, but thrice…and now you're in his blood, and he needs you…and you need to learn not to trifle with big men…bad men…"

My eyes were lolling in my head as I tried to brace for the next impact, but I relaxed myself. Then he started to choke me, hard. I felt the stifling as I tried for a breath, then attempted to will myself not to breathe, hoping to get it over before he started having his fun with me, but I couldn't. My lungs strained and I began to panic.

I tried to gasp, but couldn't. No M-Squad was coming to save me. No cops. No…Mom. I was on my own.

Completely alone.

My eyes opened and my gaze lifted over his shoulder and I saw the box in the corner, door still open, almost leering, as though it were taunting me. Now the flashbacks came, at the end, as my pitiful life waited in the balance and I remembered moments I had tried to forget. All those years, Mom had held me in this house, like Wolfe was holding me now, keeping me captive, slowly squeezing the life out of me – and I let her, afraid of the box. Years of helpless imprisonment, putting aside everything I wanted out of my life.

It taunted me, in that corner. Years of being stuck in it,

trapped, helpless.

Emotions poured over me like the icy water that had hit me earlier, a sudden, sharp shock. I remembered the last time I was stuck in that metal coffin, days without getting a breath of fresh air, and my fear built and built until I exploded, anger and hatred and sadness all rushing out. I pounded on the metal of the door, put everything into it and felt something I had never felt in all the times I had been in there.

It moved. The door moved, just a little. I hit it again and again and it budged a little more, and a crack of light from the outside peeked in. I hammered at the door, kicked, pushed at it, screaming, grunting, my weary and cramped muscles crying out to get free. The corner bent enough that I could stick my fingers through, and I pushed and the metal bent as I applied more and more pressure. With a final kick and punch I heard the top and bottom hinges strain and break and I ripped the door free, sucking in the breaths of life and falling to the basement floor, the cold concrete and breathable air letting me know that I was alive, and for once...I wasn't helpless.

I wasn't.

I stared back at Wolfe's soulless eyes and the same fury washed over me, the same desperate hunger for air and life. He held me at arm's length and my bare hands came up of their own accord and surged forward, wrapping themselves around his hairy neck. The black eyes looked at me in surprise and a smile found its way to his lips. His grip tightened on me as mine tightened on his neck. There was no way I would be able to kill him before he killed me, I knew that. And I didn't care. I would not die without him knowing that I wasn't a helpless, defenseless little doll just here for him to play with.

My fingers dug into his throat and he laughed. "You're going to have to squeeze much harder than that to make Wolfe feel it, my little doll. All you're doing is giving Wolfe a case of the tingles."

I gripped him tighter and he squeezed me so hard my head pushed back. I worried for a moment it was going to pop off, but I maintained my furious hold on him. I could feel a tingle of my own in my hands, likely from the fact that he was depriving my brain of oxygen. I dug my fingernails into his skin and I saw faint trickles of blood well up beneath them, even as I started to feel a sensation of lightheadedness percolate through my being.

"What...what are you...doing...?" Wolfe's words were choked, his eyes wide. I felt his grip slacken on my neck. I didn't dare loosen mine, and the lightheadedness I had experienced was growing into something more. The light in the room seemed to be brightening, amplifying.

"It...it BURNS!" He let out a howl of pain and batted at my hands. His claws dug into my wrists, scratching at them, drawing more blood that trickled down his fingers. I looked down to see it pooling in little drips on the concrete and then looked back to his face, awash in agony, and felt his weight start to drag me down. My hands were clutching his throat; my skin was hot and my head was throbbing, rushing with blood. I felt a heightened sense of...everything.

I suddenly realized the room reeked of blood and fear, and I drew in another sharp breath. Faint thumping noises upstairs were audible to me for the first time, and I could hear noises in the pipes and sirens blocks away, and all this over the whimpering and screaming of Wolfe. My skin was on fire with the heat of his throat in my hands, and I could feel the veins in Wolfe's neck pumping blood past my fingers.

"PLEASE!!" His voice shrieked, begging, pleading, filling the air in the basement. It was at that moment that I realized that if he could speak, I wasn't choking him – at least not effectively. "It hurts...SO...MUCH!" His words came out in a whimpering shriek. "Wolfe is sorry, little doll, please let him go, please-

pleaseplease…"

A few more wails of agony, one last whimper, and a death rattle filled the air. I held Wolfe by the neck and there was a bitter taste in my mouth as he went slack; his black eyes rolled back in his head, now truly lifeless. The lightheaded sensation filled me and I felt like I was floating, then flying, but not like I had when I went unconscious…instead it was like I was flying at a hundred miles an hour, even though I was still there in the basement, looking at Wolfe's dead eyes.

Though he weighed several hundred pounds, I held him up by the neck for several minutes, afraid to let go and empowered by the rush of whatever it was that was causing my head to spin. I finally let him slip from my grasp, and his body fell back, knocking over the box, which landed on the ground with a horrendous crash. Wolfe's body rolled off the side of it and slid to the floor, unmoving.

I took two steps back and slumped against the wall. My head felt like it was about to explode. My mind was so jumbled I couldn't control it; leaping in every direction, thoughts I could not have conceived of just a few minutes earlier were dashing through my head so quickly I couldn't even track them all.

I looked back at the two objects of my greatest fear and a heady feeling settled over me. I kicked Wolfe's shin with an outstretched leg. He didn't budge, didn't blink. He was dead.

And I was free.

Twenty-four

I leaned against the wall, trying to catch my breath as thoughts whirled in my head. The creak of a floorboard focused me. I saw a foot appear at the top of the steps and tried to stand, then collapsed when I saw whose foot it was.

Reed tiptoed down the stairs and froze when he caught sight of Wolfe, then charged down the last few steps after he saw me, dropping to his knees at my side. "Sienna!"

"Yes?" I looked back at him, still wobbly.

"Thank God you're alive, you look..." He frowned in concern and his hand patted my forehead. "Uh...you...uh..."

"I think Wolfe did a number on me before I killed him," I replied through bloody lips.

He nodded agreement, looking somewhat gray in the face. He shifted from me and eased over to Wolfe on his knees and felt the monster's cheek. He looked back to me with an expression of fear and amazement. "He's dead."

"I just said that," I replied with an eye roll that left me feeling like my entire brain had done a backflip.

Reed shifted back to me. "I didn't believe you." His hands went to my neck and I felt the pressure of his touch for a few minutes; then he raised them in front of my eyes, covered in blood. "To answer your earlier question, yes, he did a number on you."

"Not the first time," I replied with a grunt. "But it's the last." I laughed, a light, airy laugh that turned into a hacking cough. Ouch.

He placed a hand on my forehead. "You're burning up." He

tossed a look at Wolfe's body, then back to me. "How did you kill him?"

"I don't know…I just grabbed him around the throat and held on."

"So you strangled him?" His hand was resting on my forehead, as though he was trying to take my temperature.

"No…" I thought back to my hands around his throat, about him talking to me, pleading for his life. "He was still talking, so I couldn't have choked him to death."

Without warning, Reed yanked his hand away from me and toppled backward to the floor. He shook for a moment and stretched out as though he were convulsing. Crawling on my hands and knees, I moved toward him. "Are you all right?" I asked as he bucked once more and pulled himself to a sitting position. I reached out a hand and he batted it away, hard. I looked at him and his brown eyes came up at me laden with suspicion, a haggard look etched on his face, which was suddenly worn.

"Don't…touch me." His voice was violent, edgy.

I reached out again and he slid away in a hurry, hitting his back against the wall and sliding to his feet, looking down on me, his chest heaving as though he were fighting for a breath. "I said DON'T TOUCH ME!"

"What…is it?" I looked up at him from the floor, stunned at his sudden change in persona.

"Don't you get it?" He slid against the wall, moving toward the stairwell, still leaning against it for support. "You killed Wolfe…with your touch."

"What?" I asked, horrified. I looked at my hands and back to Reed, who had a look of revulsion on his face. "What…what am I?" A concern grew in me as I tried to wrap my still reeling mind around what had happened.

There was a sound upstairs, the noise of a door exploding open. Reed looked up and back to me, then took two steps toward a basement window and broke through it, springing with amazing agility through the hole and leaving a pile of broken, white-covered glass on the floor behind him.

The door to the basement flew open and heavy footfalls came down the stairs. I struggled to my feet once more, looking at my hands, wondering if what Reed said was true and if I would have to use them again on whoever was coming after me.

I breathed a sigh of relief when Old Man Winter appeared at the top of the steps. He took a quick look at Wolfe, then called up the stairs, "Sienna is all right and…Wolfe is dead." He hurried down the last few steps to me, followed by a half dozen agents, all of whom goggled at the body of Wolfe, laying supine on the cold concrete floor next to the overturned box.

I braced myself against the wall as the agents formed a semi-circle around Wolfe and Old Man Winter stooped next to him. Ariadne came down last, followed by two more figures; Dr. Perugini and Dr. Sessions. Ariadne made her way over to me, following Dr. Perugini. Sessions made his way to Wolfe's corpse.

"No pulse, but no sign of trauma…" I heard Dr. Sessions rattle off as he leaned over Wolfe. "Are we sure he's dead?"

Sessions cast a look at Old Man Winter, who nodded. "He would not lie down like this. He is dead."

"I need you to sit down, sweetie." Dr. Perugini's thickly accented words washed over me and she and Ariadne eased closer, each going to one of my elbows.

"DON'T TOUCH ME!" I screamed at them, the thought of Reed's words still hanging in my mind. They both jumped back a step when I exploded, and I held my hands out to put them at arm's length.

"I don't get it; I see no cause of death." Dr. Sessions' words felt like an indictment of me.

"I killed him," I said into the silence that filled the room. "I killed him with my touch…"

Ariadne and Dr. Perugini exchanged a look. "If you say so," Dr. Perugini said with an air of patronization. She reached for me again, Ariadne a step behind her. "I need you to sit down and relax…"

Old Man Winter took two long strides from where he stood at the side of Wolfe's body and landed a long arm on the shoulders of Dr. Perugini and Ariadne. "Don't…" he mumbled in quiet warning, "…touch her."

They both looked at him in surprise, but Perugini's turned to annoyance. "She's injured. I need to get her back to the Directorate and treat her wounds."

Old Man Winter did not budge. "She'll be fine. Do not touch her without heavy gloves." His gaze fell over me again, and he turned back to where the agents stood around the body of Wolfe.

"Or what?" Perugini spat at him. "She's hurt, she's delusional, Erich! She's just been through a ridiculous level of trauma – you can't possibly think she killed this maniac by touching him." She looked after him, and he hesitated, and the chill of the cold air from the window filled the room, swirling around him as though it were embracing a very old friend. "Erich?" she asked again, note of disbelief filling her voice. "You don't actually believe her?"

He stared down at Wolfe for a long moment before he answered. "Certainly I believe her," he replied. His cold blue eyes swept back to Dr. Perugini, then to Ariadne, finally coming to rest on me. "It is as she said. She touched him, and he likely screamed and begged for his life, and she killed him with her hands. With her touch."

I felt a chill unrelated to the broken window as my eyes followed Old Man Winter's down to the corpse of Wolfe, the scariest maniac I'd ever heard of, dead, helpless, on the floor – the way I'd made him. I looked back up and the biting fear ate at me, doubts, horror, still swirling in my brain, which was rocketing at a mile a second. "What…am…I?" I croaked out at him.

"What am I?" I asked again, stronger this time. He did not answer me, instead turning away after gesturing at Wolfe's body as he swept up the stairs. Dr. Perugini reached for my elbow and I brushed her off, knocking her aside.

"WHAT AM I?" I howled at him as he retreated.

A voice, deathly familiar, prickled at the back of my mind, instilling a sense of calm that came from deep inside, an answer to a question that was asked and answered somewhere in the depths of me.

Soul eater, it said in a raspy, whispering voice.

Succubus.

Twenty-five

"You're what would be known in mythology as a succubus," Dr. Sessions said in a voice pitched with excitement. We were back at the Directorate hours later. I had let Ariadne and Dr. Perugini coax me upstairs and into a waiting car after my question was answered from within. Although I was familiar with the myth of succubi, I knew that the answer hadn't come from me. And that left another question that I was sure I could answer, but didn't want to.

After a visit to the medical unit to make sure I was all right, Ariadne had asked me to see Dr. Sessions. I'd agreed. So there I sat, clad once more in a long sleeved turtleneck, jeans, and with a pair of heavy mittens they'd rummaged for me, on his examination table, him keeping an arm's length away while he talked.

"I thought that succubi…uh…" I blushed as I thought about having to ask the doctor the question that was on my mind. Ariadne and Dr. Perugini were both in the lab as well, hovering in the background. Perugini, in particular, looked as though she was ready to level Dr. Sessions, staring at him from across the room through half-slitted eyes. "…slept with men in order to steal their souls."

Dr. Sessions smiled, which at the present moment didn't creep me out as much as it might have a week ago. "No. Well," he rescinded, "you could, I suppose, but all that's necessary is the touch of your skin. You touch someone with your bare hands, or your face – anything involving flesh to flesh contact, and they'll start to feel the effects of your power."

"Mom knew," I said in a low whisper. "That's why she had rule #4."

"Excuse me?" Sessions looked at me.

"My mom," I explained. "She had a rule that I wasn't allowed to wander around the house without being fully dressed, down to having on gloves at all times. I assumed that it was because we had to be ready to run at a moment's notice."

"Yes, your mother likely knew," he agreed, turning back to some printouts of the data he'd accumulated on me through our testing. "She was probably the source of your power; I suspect she was a succubus as well. It's very rare, of course; most of our data on succubi is apocryphal – in fact, there's only one in our records known to be alive." He chirruped with a twitter of excitement. "Well, three now, I suppose, counting you and your mother."

"How…do I kill someone by touching them?" I asked, still in disbelief.

"Looking for a scientific explanation?" He shrugged, still an air of whimsical amusement, as though he were so excited by the prospect of a new subject for study that he failed to realize that I might be feeling something other than what he was. "I can't explain it without studying the effect in more detail. Of course, we brought Wolfe's body back for study—" he pointed to a white sheet on a nearby table, covering a monstrous corpse—"which should be just a wealth of information. Since this is the first chance anyone's had to study a confirmed victim of a succubus, it's really a pioneering step…"

Victim. His words drifted past me after that, and as he kept talking, I thought about Wolfe as a victim. Wolfe had never been a victim of anything in his life until I came along. He made victims; he wasn't one. Until now.

Now he was my first.

"…so I'll be studying him. Of course there are tests I'll be wanting to run on you as time goes by, and hopefully we can get to the bottom of the root physiological causes of your power." Sessions clapped his hands together and looked at me with unsuppressed glee. "It's very exciting, isn't it?"

I cast a look back at Wolfe, still hidden under the sheet. "Thrilling."

It is thrilling, isn't it…

I ignored the voice in my head and turned back to Dr. Sessions. "A question about succubi…aren't they supposed to drain the souls of their victims?"

He entertained a high, giggly laugh. "Yes, according to anecdotes, incubi – the male counterpart of your type of meta – and succubi steal the souls of their victims, but of course they also are reported to do it through sexual contact, which is not what happened in this case." He pushed his glasses up on his nose, suddenly disheveled. "Right?"

A wave of revulsion passed over me. "I grabbed him around the throat, Doc."

"Oh, okay, that's what I thought." He recovered and shifted back to glee. "I think it doubtful you 'stole his soul'," Sessions said with a scornful laugh. "Bear in mind that also in the mythological descriptions is the idea that a succubus or incubus comes to their victim in their dreams, which is," he said with another giggle, "absolutely preposterous."

I stared back at him. "Right."

"I think you can see the myth and reality when it comes to meta-humans is somewhat divergent." He smiled. "Any other questions? Very good, then. Well, you get back to recovering under Dr. Perugini's able ministrations and I'll give you a call as soon as I have anything of interest to report."

"Doctor," I said as I stood. "This power…" He stared back at me, curious as to what I was going to ask. "Does this mean I'm never going to be able to touch anyone…ever?"

"Through heavy clothing you can. We'll need to do some study, but I suspect that there's a certain thickness of material that will prevent bleedthrough of your powers." He adjusted his glasses once more.

"I meant with my skin." My mouth was dry, but I didn't need a drink.

Well...no, I...I think not," he stuttered. "We'll research the effect further, but it seems that if you killed Wolfe with your touch, then it will have the same effect on anyone else you happen to be in contact with." He seemed satisfied with his answer until he looked over my shoulder. I turned in time to see Dr. Perugini shaking her head in disgust and Sessions amended, "But...we need to do more research to be certain."

Dr. Perugini made a rattling sound of annoyance in her throat and reached up to place her hand on my back, avoiding touching the skin. Ariadne walked next to me and we descended into the underground tunnel back to the HQ building.

"So," Ariadne began, "now that Wolfe is out of the picture, have you given any thought to your next move?"

"Not really."

"You could stay here," Ariadne answered, pushing a lock of hair behind her ear.

"I don't have anywhere else to go," I replied, "so I suppose I will for now."

"I meant long-term," she corrected. "Our facilities and resources for meta-humans are unparalleled. We can help you learn how to control and harness your power."

Control and harness, two words that mean they'd like to make you their willing slave...

"Can we please focus on getting her to the point where she's no longer badly wounded before we start talking about anything else?" Dr. Perugini's irritation finally broke loose, causing Ariadne to do as the doctor ordered. Parting ways with us at the medical unit, Ariadne promised to stop by again later to check on me. Dr. Perugini walked me back to my bed, filling the air with florid Italian curses. I doubt she realized I knew them.

"Rest," Perugini commanded before she disappeared into her office. I lay back, resting my head on the pillow following the doctor's exhortation, and glanced around the medical unit. The curtains were down and the bay was empty.

They want to own you...they want to make you their property...run while you can...

"I can't yet," I said, voice no higher than a whisper. "I need answers."

They don't want to give you answers; they want you to work for them, to...kill for them.

I snorted, staring into the steel wall opposite my bed. "Let me ask you something...where's my mom?"

I don't know. And if I did, I wouldn't tell you.

"You're lying."

"Excuse me?"

I looked up, startled. Dr. Perugini had appeared from her office door and crossed the bay. "Who were you talking to?"

I tried to keep my expression blank. "Myself. Bad habit, I'm afraid. It's what happens," I said with a light chuckle, "when you have no one but Mom to talk to for years and years."

"Ah," she said. Her face bore discomfort and I could tell she felt sorry for me. "Here you go; something to dull the pain." She dropped two pills into my outstretched hand and reached to the side table where a pitcher of water sat, poured me a glass and handed it over. She watched as I dropped the pills in my mouth and drank half a glass. "Anything else I can do for you?"

"No," I said.

"You'll be healed by tomorrow. Nasty marks on your neck should all be gone by then. Skull fracture too; it's already almost knitted together."

"Thank you." I mouthed the words, not sure if I really meant them. I felt a sudden urge to hit her, to beat her bloody and then slam her head in the door until she stopped moving, and then...

"Are you sure you're all right?" Dr. Perugini looked at me, eyes searching mine.

I looked at the blank steel plating that covered the wall across from my bed, the shiny, reflective surface, then looked back at her with a practiced smile. "I'm fine. Just a little tired, that's all. And my head hurts. It's been a long day."

"Of course. I'll leave you alone. Just call out if you need anything." With a smile, she turned and went back into her office, closing the door behind her.

You wanted to do it, to beat her, to kill her…

"No, I didn't," I whispered, softer this time.

You did; I felt it; you're coming around to my way of thinking…

"No." I stared at the wall, and I could see just the faintest image of myself. "Tell me where my mother is."

Told you. Don't know…and I wouldn't tell you if I did.

Somewhere in her office, Dr. Perugini must have hit the light switch, because the medical unit was bathed in darkness, broken only by the faint light of instrument panels. I looked back at the steel, mirrored surface across from me and my face was gone, replaced by black eyes and teeth that looked unusually sharp; predatory, even. I smiled, and my voice came out harsher, lower and more rasping than usual.

"We'll see about that…Wolfe."

About the Author

Robert J. Crane was born and raised on Florida's Space Coast before moving to the upper midwest in search of cooler climates and more palatable beer. He graduated from the University of Central Florida with a degree in English Creative Writing. He worked for a year as a substitute teacher and worked in the financial services field for seven years while writing in his spare time. He makes his home in the Twin Cities area of Minnesota.

He can be contacted in several ways:

Via email at cyrusdavidon@gmail.com

Follow him on Twitter - **@robertJcrane**

Connect on Facebook – **robertJcrane (Author)**

Website – **robertJcrane.com**

The Sanctuary Series
Epic Fantasy by Robert J. Crane

The world of Arkaria is a dangerous place, filled with dragons, titans, goblins and other dangers. Those who live in this world are faced with two choices: live an ordinary life or become an adventurer and seek the extraordinary.

Defender
The Sanctuary Series, Volume One

Cyrus Davidon leads a small guild in the human capital of Reikonos. Caught in an untenable situation, facing death in the den of a dragon, they are saved by the brave fighters of Sanctuary who offer an invitation filled with the promise of greater adventure. Soon Cyrus is embroiled in a mystery - someone is stealing weapons of nearly unlimited power for an unknown purpose, and Sanctuary may be the only thing that stands between the world of Arkaria and total destruction.

Available Now!

Avenger
The Sanctuary Series, Volume Two

When a series of attacks on convoys draws suspicion that Sanctuary is involved, Cyrus Davidon must put aside his personal struggles and try to find the raiders. As the attacks worsen, Cyrus and his comrades find themselves abandoned by their allies, surrounded by enemies, facing the end of Sanctuary and a war that will consume their world.

Available Now!

Savages
A Sanctuary Short Story

Twenty years before Cyrus Davidon joined Sanctuary, his father was killed in a war with the trolls and he has never forgiven them. Enter Vaste, a troll unlike most; courageous, loyal and an outcast. When Cyrus and Vaste become trapped in a far distant land, they are forced to overcome their suspicions and work together to get home.

Available Now!

Champion
The Sanctuary Series, Volume Three

As the war heats up in Arkaria, Vara is forced to flee after an ancient order of skilled assassins infiltrates Sanctuary and targets her. Cyrus Davidon accompanies her home to the elven city of Termina and the two of them become embroiled in a mystery that will shake the very foundations of the Elven Kingdom – and Arkaria.

Coming this Spring!

A Familiar Face
A Sanctuary Short Story

Cyrus Davidon gets more than he bargained for when he takes a day away from Sanctuary to visit the busy markets of his hometown, Reikonos. While there, he meets a woman who seems very familiar, and appears to know him, but that he can't place.

Coming this Summer!

Untouched
The Girl in the Box, Book 2

Still haunted by her last encounter with Wolfe and searching for her mother, Sienna Nealon must put aside her personal struggles when a new threat emerges – Aleksandr Gavrikov, a metahuman so powerful, he could destroy entire cities – and he's focused on bringing the Directorate to its knees.

Coming Summer 2012!

Soulless
The Girl in the Box, Book 3

Coming Summer 2012!

SAMANTHA'S PROMISE

Nicholas J. Ambrose

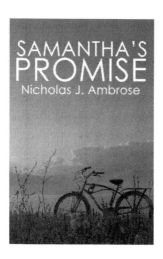

After a long and stressful week, capped by a thunderstorm and attracting the unwanted attention of a man in a bar, Samantha is too strung up to take Imogen, her younger sister, cycling. So she does the next best thing: she makes a promise to do it next weekend instead.

As the weeks pass, though, Samantha's promise fails to materialise, slipping further and further away until she has almost forgotten about it. After all, there's always next week – and Imogen can go alone if she's that desperate.

But unbeknownst to Samantha, next week might never come. Because there's something very, very wrong with Imogen – and the ten-year-old's time is quickly running out.

Available on **Kindle** now
Carry on reading for the opening chapter!

Made in the USA
Middletown, DE
04 May 2023

30056424R00102